The Truth Shall Set You Free

Bev,
It has been a joy knowing
you over the years as
a wonderful friend.
Hope you enjoy this story.
God bless you.
Love, Shirley

The Truth Shall Set You Free

SHIRLEY KALPIN-OLSON

To order additional copies of this book, contact:
Xlibris Corporation
1-888-795-4274
www.Xlibris.com
Orders@Xlibris.com
27632

Contents

Chapter 1: Is This Really My Sister?............................9

Chapter 2: Tiffany's Reunion with Her Brother....................13

Chapter 3: Tiffany's New Home.........................17

Chapter 4: Tiffany's Story............................21

Chapter 5: Escape to a Safe House....................25

Chapter 6: Mom's Near Death.........................29

Chapter 7: Mom's New Husband.....................33

Chapter 8: Train Ride for the Runaway...................39

Chapter 9: Alone in Orlando.......................43

Chapter 10: Tiffany's First Job.....................49

Chapter 11: Mom's Tragic Death....................53

Chapter 12: Another Escape......................67

Chapter 13: From Riches to Rags....................77

Chapter 14: In Need of Help!....................85

Chapter 15: Tiffany's Nightmares......................91

Chapter 16: The Truth Is Found to Set Us Free...................95

Dedication

"I would like to dedicate this story to all my children, grandchildren and great grandchildren. I would like to Thank: My writing friend Audrey for her help and critiques, my husband, Jim for his encouragement and understanding and most of all, my Precious Savior Jesus, who has been the inspiration for this story."

Chapter 1

Is This Really My Sister?

Pastor Paul, handsome, with dark twinkling eyes, was sitting in the church office when he received the phone call that was to change his life. He answered the phone in his usual way, "Hello, this is Pastor Paul, may I help you?"

There was a long pause as he heard on the other end, "I . . . I read your article in the *Miami Herald* about your place for homeless people. I think I can use your help." A stammering voice was heard.

"You are certainly welcome to come here, we will help you. Can you tell me your name, and where are you, right now?" Pastor Paul continued.

"M . . . my name is T . . . Tiffany, I saw your picture and I . . . I think I might be your s . . . sister. I am in Miramar, northwest of Miami." the voice over the phone said with hesitation.

Paul gasped as he heard the name Tiffany, his heart started pounding. "Tiffany, is this really you? Are you really my sister?"

"Y . . . Yes, I . . . I think that I might be. When I noticed you picture, it looked a lot like a picture of my brother my mother gave me before she died. I wish I could meet you. I have been looking for you for many years; I sure hope you are my brother. All I can think of is the times you helped me when I was little, so very long ago."

"I have been praying for you since we were separated. Are . . . are you okay? I am very anxious to see and meet with you."

It had been fourteen years since Dad and I had seen or heard from my sister. So many times we had tried to find her but always came to a dead-end. It was as if she and Mom had left the face of this earth. I have been praying for her since I learned how to pray. One day, as I was praying, the Lord said to me, "The truth will set your sister free, and you will see her soon." This same voice kept coming to me every time I prayed for my sister. I trusted God, so I never gave up hope.

Paul's mind came back to reality as he said, "I feel that you are my sister, and I want you to come here as soon as you can. Is there a Greyhound bus station near where you are?"

"Yes, I saw one about 2 miles from where I am now. I don't have any money, so I don't know how I can get there."

"If you can leave there soon, I will arrange a ticket in your name, to be picked up at the station for tomorrow morning."

"That would be so very nice of you. I don't want you to go out of your way for me, but I would love to see you. Is there a place we can meet? I don't think you will recognize me. I will recognize you by your picture."

"After you get off the bus, there is a small restaurant next door to the bus station. Wait there and I will come and find you. I am so thankful that God is bringing you back to me. I have been searching for you for so long. The bus leaves the station at nine in the morning. I hope that this time will not be too early for you. I will be looking forward to meeting you around noon tomorrow. Ah . . . I . . . I love you." Paul said as an afterthought, with tears streaming down his cheeks.

"I . . . I love you also, Paul, I have missed you so very much." Tiffany said, her hands shaking as she replaced the phone in the cradle. Her heart pounding so hard she could hardly breathe. She had been waiting for this day for so long.

Paul sat back and thanked God. "I know you answer prayers. Please let this be my sister and not another hoax or dead-end."

The next morning, Pastor Paul hurried to the restaurant near the Orlando bus depot. He sat in a booth near the entrance so he could see the people as they entered the restaurant. As he waited, he nervously ran his hands through his wavy hair, in expectation of seeing his lost sister. His brown eyes twinkled as his mind flashed back to when he and his sister were growing up. *She was the sweetest three-year-old, with dark brown eyes and a bush of beautiful auburn hair starting to curl around her delicate round face. He was twelve years old at this time. She was the cutest when she would get into trouble. Her dark eyes, filling with tears, amused him, as she would always look to him for comfort. He was the one she would always turn to for help. He would help her, and she would award him with part of her orange she would sneak out of the refrigerator. She was born so many years after him, but they were always very close the little time they had together.*

His eyes clouded, as he continued thinking. *Dad was gone so much on business trips that Mom became very lonely. She started drinking and running around and getting in deeper with the drug scene. I would take care of my sister most of the time when I would come home from school. I tried to tell Mom to get help, but she wasn't able to.*

One day after school, I was anxious to see Dad, as he was coming home that night from one of his business trips. When I arrived into the house, I immediately sensed something terribly wrong. I could see that Mom's bags were packed, and she had Tiffany by the hand and was heading out the door. Dad was sitting in his chair with a stunned and solemn look on his face. I asked, "What is going on here? What's wrong? Where are you going, Mom?" This frightened me, as I realized what was happening. I could remember my dear sister tugging on my arm as she sobbed. "I don't want to leave my brother and Dad.

Please, Mom, let us be a family." Then all of a sudden, she was swept away from me. It was as if the wind was sucked out of me.

Mom had informed my dad that she felt he could take care of me better and that she had found someone else who would take care of her and Tiffany. She needed to go away to find an easier life for herself. I was very angry at my mom at that time. As she reached out to hug me, I still remembered pushing her away from me. Tears ran down his face as he was remembering all the hurt and sadness since his parents' divorce.

My dad later showed me how to find God, which helped me out in my life. I was very grateful to him. Since then, as a minister, God has been with me, and I have used this time to try to help homeless people and others who maybe going through some of the tragedies we did as a family. I have been praying for God to help my sister and my mom also.

Paul's mind came back to the present as he sat in his booth at the restaurant near the entrance, watching the people come in. He noticed only one young man with short auburn hair covered by an old floppy hat and wearing baggy clothes push a backpack into the booth next to his. As he sat down, he appeared to be looking around.

Disappointed, Paul thought, "That can't be my sister, this is a fellow." Paul decided to go over to the young man and ask him if he noticed a young lady on the bus with him matching the description he remembered her as. Just as he worked his way over to the young man, he got up out of his booth, came toward him with his arm outstretched, holding an orange. Paul finally found his lost sister.

Chapter 2

Tiffany's Reunion with Her Brother

It was a sweltering day in June when Tiffany ambled into the small cafe next to the bus station Paul had told her to meet him. She plopped her backpack down and squeezed her dingy body into a booth as the sweat poured from her brow. She was starving and hoping to bargain for a glass of iced tea. She had only a few pennies to her name.

As she sat savoring the free tea, she took out her favorite picture. It was a picture of her brother, which she had gotten from her mother before her tragic death. She had kept it sacred over the years. Staring at this picture, her mind swept back to the past. *She could still see her brother and father's eyes filled with tears as her mom grabbed her hand and whisked her out the door away from her brother whom she had loved more than anyone.*

If she could be united with her brother, she could be rest assured he would help her. Spending her seventeenth birthday all alone, sleeping on a park bench, had caused her to be extremely depressed. She had been through so many difficulties her mind wouldn't let her believe she may be finding her brother, *What if this fellow isn't your brother? If he is, what if he doesn't like your looks, you're not exactly a lovely fair maiden dressed like a boy.* Tiffany wished she felt secure enough to get rid of the boy garb, but she didn't even have any girl clothes. She was still disguised as a boy, Samuel, although she yearned to go back to being herself. This was not a possibility, for she was so afraid of Frank and his men, who was still lurking out there somewhere searching for her. She knew that if they found her, and her knowing too much about their criminal activities, he and his cronies would probably kill her, just like they did her mother. She just hoped that her brother would accept her as she is, if indeed this man was her brother.

Tiffany's thoughts depressed her, but the idea of possibly seeing her brother again was causing happy tears to fall from her face.

Things are going to be different now, she vowed. Seeing Paul again was going to be wonderful, she had at least a slim glimmer of hope. She knew he would protect her. Remembering how she always gave him a treat when he would help her, she figured she had to have something to give him when she met him again. She reached inside her backpack and brought out an orange she had saved.

As Tiffany anxiously waited with tears falling, she could barely see others in the restaurant. Suddenly she spied a good-looking, well-dressed man in a booth nearby, peering around as if looking for someone. "That fellow looks like the picture in the newspaper. He must be my brother," she said to no one as her heart started pounding.

Tiffany, grabbing the orange, slid cautiously out of the booth. Realizing that this man didn't recognize her, she quickly removed her floppy hat and let down her hair. As she awkwardly walked toward Paul, she suddenly felt so much shame and guilt coming from her past that she could barely lift up her eyes to look at him. She felt very unsure of herself at that moment, as she slowly held out the orange to him.

All of a sudden, she could see that Paul had recognized her as her curls swirled around her face. She knew that he was indeed her brother.

When Tiffany was finally able to look Paul directly into his eyes, she said, "I am Tiffany. I believe I'm your sister. I have been hoping and praying that you would truly be my brother." Tiffany was not sure what he would say or do. She knew that she would eventually have to tell him about their mother and all the details, but right now, she just wanted her brother to hold her like he used to so many years ago.

Seeing Tiffany's pain and awkwardness, Paul met her midway and said as he cautiously drew her into his arms, "You are my Tiffany. I am so happy you are here. I have missed you so much."

"I am so happy to see you again," Tiffany said. The tears continued to stream down her cheeks as she felt the comforting arms of her brother encircle her. She hung on to her brother as if she was going to lose him again. The sweat of her unbathed body apparently did not seem to bother him. As he hugged her back, she could feel his warm tears brush against her neck.

Tiffany was sobbing so hard, the tears left smudges down her face. As Paul tenderly wiped away the smudges, she knew in her heart that this was indeed her brother. She had not felt any love like this from any man since she was three years old. She breathed a prayer of thanksgiving to God for bringing them back together.

Paul was also praying, "Thank you, Jesus, for bringing my sister back to me. Help us to bring her twinkle back into her eyes. I can see in her eyes the suffering she has gone through."

Chapter 3

Tiffany's New Home

When Paul and Tiffany arrived at his house in Buena Vista, he introduced her to his wife and children.

Maria, Paul's wife, hugged her newfound sister-in-law and said, "It is so good to finally meet you. Paul has been looking and praying for you for so many years. I am so glad that God has finally brought you together."

Tiffany hugged her sister-in-law as she said, "I am so grateful to be reunited with you all. I have never had a real family since I was very small. I don't feel worthy being here, I feel so grubby. Is there a chance I could freshen up a little and borrow an old pants or shirt to wear until I can get some clothes?"

"Yes, of course. You can have a fresh relaxing bath as I lay out some clean clothes for you near the tub. I am sure that my clothes will fit you, as we are about the same size, You are welcome to wear anything you want until we can get some for you."

As Maria led Tiffany to get cleaned up, Pastor Paul knelt on his knees in thanksgiving to God. "Thank you, Lord, for bringing my sister back to me. Help me to do the best I can to help her get to know you as the truth that will set her free. I can see that she will need much love and kindness, which we aim to give her with your help. Amen."

Tiffany was so very grateful for the love and charity offered. She said, "Thank you both for taking me in, I would always remember this day. I haven't had a nice warm bath for many days, and it will feel so good."

"After you get cleaned up, we will have dinner, unless you want to rest first," Maria said.

Tiffany's stomach growled as she smelled the wonderful aroma coming from the kitchen. She hadn't had a real meal in so many days; she couldn't remember the last one. "I can hardly wait to eat; I smell such delicious aromas. I will be done with my bath and dressed in just a wink."

When Tiffany arrived downstairs, she felt like a queen. She loved the blouse and skirt she had found beside the tub. She finally felt like a woman again as she took the bandage off her breasts that she had worn for such a long time. She felt a wonderful sense of freedom. She was so thankful for her brother and sister-in-law.

At the table, the mashed potatoes, gravy, wonderful meatloaf, vegetables, and all the trimmings gave off such a aroma, she could hardly contain herself. Tiffany had not had a real meal like this for eight months. She didn't want to make a pig out of herself, but she felt like she could eat the whole meal by herself.

She looked up from her plate with her mouth watering to start to dig in when she noticed her nephew and niece smiling at her. They were both so polite and sweet. Eight-year-old Stan, who had the handsome features of his father, was the oldest. He looked like his dad, but he also had some resemblance to someone else she knew. It was odd that he had

the same name as someone who had befriended her during her trials.

Tiffany was surprised at the wisdom and knowledge Stan seemed to have when he prayed, "Thank you, God, for the food placed before us and also for bringing our aunt back to us."

Allison was three years old. Her brown curls swirled around her brow as she cuddled up to Tiffany. If she hadn't known better, she could see herself as she looked as a child.

After the prayer, all the food was passed around, and they were all so pleasant to her as they ate. She could not remember such warmth expressed. She was elated.

After the wonderful meal, Tiffany said to Paul, while clearing the table, "You have such a wonderful and delightful family. Your children remind me of when we were little, before I was taken away from you and Dad."

Tears dropped from Paul's eyes as he hugged his sister and said, "Yes, I have always remembered those days in my heart. Dad and I have always wanted the best for you and have hoped and prayed that you would have a good life. I have also prayed that you will be able to get some of the good feelings back into your life."

Tiffany knew she was going to love her new family. She had longed for a family for so long. She felt that Paul and his god, which he talked so much about, would eventually help her get rid of all the fears, hate, and anger, which she had tucked away inside her for so many years. She wanted to learn how to trust again.

"Let us go into the living room and get comfortable and I want you to tell us all about what happened after you left with Mom," Paul said as he led his sister into the next room with his arms wrapped around her waist.

When Tiffany felt more at ease, and with the love and care of her new family, she was able to relate the gory details of her twisted past.

Sobbing violently, while Paul held her in his arms, she revealed all the pain and guilt that she had held inside her for so many years. It was like releasing a time bomb. But Paul was there for her once more.

Chapter 4

Tiffany's Story

"I don't remember much about our father, as he was gone so much when I was little. I was anxious to find both you and Dad, but, Paul, you were whom I really missed," Tiffany said.

Placing his arms around Tiffany, he said, "Dad and I have been looking for you since you left also. Please continue."

"When Mom took me away, I was forced to live with her and her boyfriend Frank. At first, he was very nice to both of us. He was handsome, with dark hair. Mom used to say that he looked a lot like my dad, but to me, his blue eyes had this eerie look about them. He had an ugly scar above his bushy eyebrow, which made me wonder how the other fellow fared.

"Later, he changed for the worse, and so did Mom. I became afraid of him. We moved and changed our names so many times I didn't even know what my real name was. I hated Frank for what he was doing to Mom. I could see that she was becoming fearful of him also. She became meaner and unresponsive to others around her. She covered her fears in more drinking and using of drugs. She was not able to be the mom I needed and wanted so desperately. I had to learn at an early age to fix meals, clean house, and do the laundry for both of them, as they did so much drinking and partying.

"As I noticed these changes in Mom, I could see the sad and desolate look in her eyes. She had been so pretty with her dark auburn hair and dark eyes, which used to have a sparkle. I could tell that Frank had a lot of influence over her, and even when we would try and get away from him, he would find ways of bringing us back to him. He had a lot of power and influence with many different people who were ugly, mean, and heartless, and who seemed to enjoy hurting others. They would bring drugs and booze and wanted Mom to get drunk with them. Then when they were drunk, I never knew what they would do. Sometimes they would try to touch me in ways that I didn't think was right. Mom wasn't able to help me, especially when I needed her the most. I began to hate them all.

"I wished so often that I could have my real mom again. I remembered the game the two of us would play when I was three years old. When I was sad or did what I was told, she would place surprises in a black box and hide it on top of the cupboard in my room. She would let me crawl up on the cupboard and get it down. When she was sad, I would hide things in it for her. This was always our little secret. This game was fun because I felt close to Mom. When Mom became more depressed and sad, this game was forgotten. I missed this mom so much. I hated her lifestyle and the men who were part of it.

"Every time we moved, it was as if we were trying to hide from someone. I could never understand any of this.

"Almost every night after I went to bed, I could hear terrible fights between Mom and Frank. I learned very early to hide under my covers and pretend that this wasn't happening, that it was just the TV.

"One night, which I will never forget, I was curled up in my little safe place under my covers when things finally quieted downstairs. I was so relieved that I was able to finally doze off.

"All of a sudden, the squeaking of my door awakened me. I lay in my bed frozen. Mom did not usually come in. It had to be that dreadful man. I could hardly breathe. I was so frightened. Barely seeing him in the shadows, this ugly, vile, liquor-smelling, filthy old man came toward me. What did he want with me? He was disgustingly drunk. He forced himself into my bed and started to touch me in areas that I knew was wrong. I fought, kicked, and even bit him, but he was too strong for me. I wasn't able to do anything to stop him as he started doing these terrible things to me. Oh, I hated him so much.

"Later, he said to me in his ugly voice, 'If you ever tell anyone about this, I will kill your mom and you.'

"I was so frightened; I didn't know what to do. I wished Dad or you were there. I know that you would take care of that old 'creepy' guy. You always took care of me when I was scared. I remembered you both as being gentle, not mean and ugly like Frank."

"I'm so sorry we weren't there for you. What happened after that?" Paul said as tears remained in his eyes.

"After Frank left, I cried out, 'Paul and Dad, where are you? Come back to me. I need you now. I am so scared!' I sobbed uncontrollably, curled up on top of the bed like a baby, until I finally cried myself to sleep.

"The next morning, I knew I needed to get out of there. I splashed water on my face and put on some clean clothes, not even noticing my swollen eyes and tear-stained cheeks and bruises. I slid out my window and slithered down my tree and hurried off to school.

"When I arrived at school, the teacher asked me, 'How did you get the bruises on your arms and face?'"

"I lied and said, 'I fell off my bicycle.' I didn't even own a bicycle. I was never able to tell anyone about what happened. I felt so guilty and had so much fear and hate for Frank. I learned early to barricade my door when I would go to bed at night. I would never let anyone do that to me again.

"Since that happened, I dreaded coming home from school. Even if I were the least bit late, Frank, in a drunken rage, eyes glazed with anger, would lash out and beat me. Mom would never stand up for me, as she usually was drugged and lying on the couch.

"I stayed away from them as much as I could. Sometimes, when I would get lonely or depressed, a thought would enter my mind, 'You will find the truth, and it will set you free.' I never knew where that thought came from, but for some reason, it would always make me feel better. I sure wished I could find that truth, whatever it was."

Paul's eyes misted with anger in them as he said, "Oh, I wish I could have been there to help you."

Chapter 5

Escape to a Safe House

"When I turned nine years old, I came home from school to find Frank's car not outside our house. I was so happy. I hated him being there. I looked around and noticed our old Chevy car packed ready to go somewhere. I ran into the house, fearful for Mom. Maybe something happened to her. As I entered the house, she was there waiting for me, sober for the first time for a long time.

"'Hurry,' she said with anxiousness. 'Go and get your most treasured things and bring it down quickly; we have to leave before Frank gets back.'

"I had a million questions, but I did as I was told and ran upstairs and brought down the little black box that meant so much to me. When I crawled into the car with the box, I could see tears in Mom's eyes, which I had not seen for a long time.

"We quickly drove down our street, the sun highlighting the thick green brushes and trees lined up along the way.

"I looked over at Mom and realized that something was dreadfully wrong. We had ran away several times before, but this time, I sensed a fear and anger in Mom, which was even more powerful than before.

"I had to ask, 'What happened? Did Frank hurt you real bad this time?'

"Mom looked at me with genuine tears streaming down her face and said with feeling, 'I'm so sorry for all of the things that have happened to you lately.'

"'What do you mean?' I questioned.

"'The school called me this morning, and they have suspected for some time that you have been abused. They have notified the police. I told them that I had suspected this for a while also, but I have not been able to do anything about it before.'

"'What are we going to do now? Frank always seems to find us wherever we go.'

"'The school told me about a safe house, which we are going to. We will have to change our names so Frank will not be able to find us again.'

"'But what about school? I'll have to start all over again. Are you sure we will be safe this time? I am so very scared.'

"'I think we will be safe. I have filed charges against Frank, and the police are going to try and get him for abuse and several other crimes he has done. He and his men are involved in many more things that I can never explain. Maybe they will be able to finally put him in jail so we can live with some freedom from his terrorizing.

"Tears streamed down my face as I realized that Mom was finally able to stand up for her and me. I reached over and gave her a big hug.

"She looked at me and smiled weakly. I realized she had been in a lot of fear, but I never realized she had so many traumas in her heart. I had thought that maybe she never had a heart, but now I knew that she did, and she was sincere when she said, 'I am going to try and change myself also.'

"All I could think of to say was 'Thank you, Mom, I love you.' I had never been able to truthfully say this to her before.

"Mom had a different look about her at that time. She even smiled with humor and said, 'What name should we use this time? You pick out a name.'

"I smiled back to her and said, 'Let's use the name Dawn, which means we can start all over again.'

"Mom smiled again and said, 'How could I have raised such a brilliant child? I now name you Tiffany Dawn.'

"This was the first time in a long time that Mom and I talked together like this. I hoped that this would never change."

Paul, engrossed in Tiffany's story, said, "You had to change your name to hide out, and no wonder we could never find you."

"Yes, "Tiffany continued. "We moved to a small town outside of Pittsburgh in a home that was set up to help people like us. Kind and caring people surrounded us. I could go to school and finally not have to fear coming home or that my mother and Frank would be drunk when I got home. We lived in this town for the next school year. My mother went to treatment and was able to stop her drinking and using drugs and started to be a mom again. I was so happy. We got to know some very nice people who knew how to love. We both were able to get some counseling. I finally perceived that there was more to life than living like we had so many years. I vowed that no man was ever going to hurt us again like Frank did.

"When school was almost finished that year, Mom sat me down and said, 'We will be going back home soon. I think it will be safe. They have Frank in jail, and I have to go back and testify against him so they can keep him in jail. If convicted, this time he will be in jail for many years. The police will arrange some safety for us from all his associates. We will leave when you finish school next week.'

"I was a little apprehensive. 'It will be good to get back to see my friend Annie.' I didn't have many friends but Annie who lived next to us. She was my friend for as long as we lived at the house. I missed her and was glad to get back to our little house, which we had someone stay in to keep tab of things while we were gone.

"We traveled back the next week but kept our new name. Mom went to court and testified against Frank. She told them what he had done to us. He threatened to kill us both as they hauled him off to jail for three years, which was all they were able to pin on him.

"'That is not enough for all he has put us through,' Mom stated with anger. All of a sudden, a thought came into my mind: 'We will know the truth, and the truth will set us free.' I felt secure with that saying."

"I am so very thankful God gave you this saying, because he kept us together by those words. These same words he gave to me to keep my hopes up. Please continue," Paul said.

Chapter 6

Mom's Near Death

"Life was finally starting to become more normal. Mom was trying really hard to be a good mom. It was hard, as we seldom had any money; she was unable to get any kind of work. It seemed that whenever she would get a job, her boss would say, 'We can't keep you here.' Apparently, someone was threatening the places she would apply at. Mom suspected that Frank was still influencing her even while in jail. She had to go on welfare again, and she hated to do that. This was causing her to become depressed again. That scared me, as I was afraid she would do something tragic and maybe start drinking again. I never wanted this to change again.

"One day, shortly after my eleventh birthday, when I returned home from school, I could not find Mom. I looked all around and called out, frightened, 'Mom, where are you?' She usually was somewhere in the house when I got home, or she would leave me a note. I looked all around, and I could not find a note or Mom. I was really scared now, and my thoughts went wild. What if someone got to her and hurt her.

"I ran out to the garage, frightened. There I found Mom lying so still, alongside the car. The car was still running, and the gas fumes were really strong. I quickly reached in and turned off the car. I knew that Mom needed help immediately. I remembered the school telling us that if we have smoke inhalation, we needed to open a door immediately. I ran over and opened the garage door. I then ran into the house, called 911, and yelled into the phone, 'Please come quickly, my mom might be dying from fumes from her car exhaust!'

"I quickly ran out and remembered the CPR I was taught in school. I kept pumping mom's chest. 'One and two and three and four and five. One and two and three and four and ten. One and two and three and four and fifteen. Breathe, breathe.' I kept this up until the ambulance finally arrived. Mom was starting to come to when the ambulance came. They had to take her away to the hospital. I was really scared. My friend Annie and her mom ran over when they noticed the ambulance.

"Annie's mother said to me as I stood outside stunned, not knowing what to do, 'We want you to stay with us until your mom gets better. Let's say a little prayer for her.'

I never knew how to pray before. All I could barely remember was when Dad said a prayer with me when I went to bed. I couldn't even remember that prayer anymore.

"'Please,' I pleaded, 'I would really like you to pray.'

"Annie's mom prayed as we all got down on our knees. I just followed what she did. 'Please, God, help Tiffany's mom get better, and help Tiffany get to know 'your truth' that you will be able to help her also. Amen.' Somehow, that prayer gave me a peace that Mom would be all right.

"Mom was in the hospital for several days. It was touch and go for many of these days if she would live or die.

"The doctor stated to me, 'If you hadn't come home and opened the garage door and called the ambulance when you did, your mother would not be alive now.'

"The police came to the hospital to talk with Mom when she got better. They suspected that Frank might have had someone try to hurt her. I was beginning to think that this nightmare would never end. Mom and I had to hide out again. Even with Frank in jail, it seemed that he still had power over Mom and me. I was becoming angry at society that we couldn't even have freedom from the criminals.

"While Mom was in the hospital, I stayed with Annie and her family. I could tell that their family was different from what I was used to. They seemed to have something called love, which I couldn't remember having except while I was in the safe house. They even took me to church with them. I felt wonderful sitting with them. I even pretended they were my real parents.

"I did learn one thing from all of this; it was that I could pray to a God. I didn't know too much about what good it would do, but Annie and her mother said that God loved me and that was all I needed right now. 'The truth will set us free' came through my mind again and again. This saying would always make me feel at peace.

"Later that month, the police managed to find the men responsible for Mom's tragedy. They were involved with Frank and his people. They went to trial and were placed in prison for attempted murder. Mom and I could finally find some peace. The police patrolled our home, which made me feel more secure."

Chapter 7

Mom's New Husband

"I was almost thirteen the year Mom remarried. Harry was nice to Mom and me when he first came to live with us. I started to trust him. He helped us with our bills and seemed to really like Mom. She needed a good person to help take care of her. She was still trying to stay straight and had gotten off the drugs. I began to relax and was able to enjoy my friend Annie and school for the first time that I could remember.

"We finally started getting out of debt. Harry was working days, and Mom started working the night shift. We were like a family, I thought.

"Suddenly, Harry and Mom started arguing like she and Frank did. Harry didn't like her working nights. He kept accusing her of having boyfriends. He started drinking before he would come home from work. When Mom was at work and I had gone to bed, Harry would come home drunk and try the same thing as Frank did. Then the nightmares started happening all over again. I couldn't handle this anymore. I started barricading my door again. I couldn't believe that some people could get so weird when they would drink. I didn't say anything to Mom because she seemed too happy. I vowed again that I was never going to let any man do this kind of thing to me again. I would kill him first. I was starting to hold in a lot of hate toward men.

"One day after school, my friend Annie asked me, 'If I would like to go to church with her on the following Sunday?' Being this was my fourteenth birthday, I thought Mom and Harry would let me go. I ran home that Friday night, anxious to ask them. I was glad Mom was home, as I didn't like being around Harry alone.

"'Mom,' I said as I ran into the house, 'Annie wants me to go to church with her on Sunday. Can I go?' I had never been in a church before that I could remember, except the time I had gone with Annie and her family, when I had stayed with them while Mom was in the hospital. I just remembered that everyone was so nice to me.

"Harry, coming in about that time and overhearing, reacted with anger, 'No, you are not going to church. You have to be here to help your mother. We are having company from my work on Sunday.' Mom didn't say a word.

"I could not believe that they would not even let me go to church. I started hating Harry more and more. He was starting to cause a lot of strife between Mom and me. The next morning, I didn't say anything. I had made up my mind; nothing was going to stop me from going to go to church on Sunday, even if I had to sneak out. I was getting very tired of having to deal with their stupid rules. Saturday night, I finished my chores quickly and went to bed early. When Mom went to work, I barricaded my door. I did this every night since the night Harry got drunk and entered my room. I kept my vow to never again let that man or any men like him get near me again.

"Sunday morning, I got up early and put on my best dress, which wasn't hard to find as I only had one, which was given to me by my friend Annie. I really liked it. As I looked in the mirror, I noticed that it fit well on my slender body, as I started filling out in the right places. As I peered at my appearance in the mirror, with my dark hair and dark eyes, I thought to myself for the first time in my life, I'm pretty. I would never dare wear this dress in front of Harry.

"As I started out my door quietly, a thought suddenly came to my mind; *I had better take a pair of jeans along so I can change before I get home.* I didn't want them to know I had gone to church. I ran back and grabbed a pair of jeans, threw them in a bag, and slipped quietly down the stairs, making sure that I wouldn't wake up Mom and Harry.

"As I crept past Mom's bedroom door and listened, I could hear them snoring. I slipped out the front door and ran the block to Annie's house.

"As we entered the church, people were again so friendly, and everyone told me how happy they were that I came. This made me feel so good. I was proud as I sat beside Annie and her family; I pretended that they were my family. Then, as I listened to the pastor, I heard him say, 'Jesus loves everyone, and his truth will set you free.' I was so excited to know that this person named Jesus loves me also. I knew that I had to get free, but I certainly didn't know what that truth was. I remembered that thought entering my mind many times before. What could that truth be? It sure was a mystery to me.

"When we were leaving the church, I asked Annie, 'What did the pastor mean when he said that the truth would set you free?'

"Annie said sweetly, 'He meant that Jesus loves you so much that he died for you, and if you believe in him he will set you free from sin.'

"I had more questions, but I knew that I had to get back before Mom and Harry got up. I quickly slipped into my jeans and hurried home.

"I was surprised to see them both waiting as I walked in the door. I could see that they were both very angry with me. 'Where were you? I suppose you went to that church,' Harry said sarcastically. 'You were told that you were not to go, weren't you?'

"'I needed to go; I heard about Jesus, and he will set me free,' I said with innocence and confidence.

"Harry became angry and slapped me across my face so hard that I flew across the floor and hit my head against the wall. I lay there for a minute, stunned. Then he came over and kicked me and said, 'I don't ever want you going there again, do you hear?' Mom came over and shouted at Harry, pushing him away from me, 'For Pete's sake, leave the poor girl be. Going to church wasn't bad; maybe we should try it sometime.'

"Harry leered at his wife. I could hear them start to argue again. I got up slowly and hobbled up the stairs. I just couldn't understand why Harry was so angry. I went into my room and barricaded my door and stayed in my room all day. I hated them. That was when I started planning my escape.

"The next morning, I left for school before Mom and Harry got up. I had to put on a lot of makeup to cover the bruises. I didn't want to have to explain things again at school.

The teacher noticed the bruises anyway and was asking questions again. I would lie again, 'I fell down while riding my bike.' This being my usual lie, I even started believing my own lie and that I might even have a bicycle.

"After school, as Annie and I was walking home, I told her, 'I am going away for a while, and I need to borrow your backpack. I really enjoyed going to church with you and your family. Thanks so much for asking me.'

"Annie questioned me, 'Why do you have to go? Are you having trouble at home again?'

"I lied as I said, 'I'm going to Florida to visit my brother. I'll call you sometime.'

"Annie gave me her backpack and a hug. I hurried home and slipped into my room before Mom or Harry got home.

"That night, I did everything that I was told so I wouldn't make Harry suspicious of my plans. When I got to my room to get ready to go to bed, I packed the backpack with my best clothes, which were few, and a jacket and some of my most valuable memoirs. I left the black box, which I always took before, because it didn't mean that much any more without Mom. I was never planning to come back to this place again. I hid my bag under my bed just as Mom came to my door.

"'Tiffany, can I come in? I'm so sorry about what happened yesterday, will you please forgive me?'"

"'Go away, I don't want to talk to anyone now. I don't blame you for Harry being a jerk. It's not your fault,' I said as an afterthought.

"'Okay. I have to go to work now. Maybe we can talk tomorrow. Goodbye,' Mom said, not knowing that this may be her last goodbye.

"I said, 'Goodbye, I'm really not mad at you.' I didn't want to leave with any hard feelings against Mom.

"After I heard Mom leave, I put on my clothes and shoes and grabbed a baseball bat that I had found and hid under the covers. I purposely left the door open. I knew that Harry would try to come in as he always did after we had a fight. That was his way of making up with me. But this gal was never going to make up with him again. Not in this life, I hated him so much, almost as much as I hated Frank.

"Sure enough, after things had quieted downstairs, I heard his steps outside my door. I was ready for him this time. The door squeaked open and in my room he was. I lay quietly in the bed pretending to be asleep. As he sat down on my bed and tried to crawl in, I grabbed the baseball bat and hit him so hard on the head I thought I could hear a crack.

"He groaned, made a moaning sound, and fell over. I thought that I had killed him. I didn't even check to see. I didn't even care.

"I grabbed my bag from under the bed, slipped the cash and some change out of Harry's billfold, threw the billfold back on the bed and ran out the door; I didn't even bother to look back.

"I said goodbye under my breath and hurried out the front door. I threw my house key on the ground outside our door because I figured that I was never coming back. I ran down the moonlit street. I would duck behind a tree or bush every time a car would come by. I didn't want anyone to see me. I ran until I saw the city bus coming because I didn't want to have to wait at a bus stop.

I grabbed the first bus that would take me to the train depot and was thankful that I had grabbed some cash for the fare. I walked to the backseat of the bus so I wouldn't attract attention to myself. I didn't want to talk to anyone.

"When I arrived at the train depot, I knew that a train would be leaving around 3 a.m. I had checked this out earlier. This train was leaving for Orlando, Florida, and that was my destination.

Chapter 8

Train Ride for the Runaway

"There were several people in the line getting tickets. I slid in behind a middle-aged gentleman with dark hair. He had blue eyes that twinkled when he talked, and he had just enough gray in his sideburns to make him look distinguished. He seemed very kind as he talked with me. When the lady at the window asked for a name for his ticket, I overheard him say Anderson. As the next person up, I said with confidence, 'Tiffany Anderson,' when asked for the name on my ticket. I just then adopted a dad in my mind. I had the same last name.

"I went and sat near Mr. Anderson. Just then, a policeman came over to me as I was waiting. I pretended to be reading, As he stopped in front of me, I suddenly, became fearful that they had found out about what I had done to Harry. I just knew that I was on my way to jail. My heart was beating so loudly I thought that the policeman could possibly hear it. He looked at me and asked, 'Aren't you a little young to be out here by yourself this late?'

"'I'm with my father, over there.' I motioned toward Mr. Anderson. 'We're on our way to Orlando to go to Disney World,' I lied. Thank goodness Mr. Anderson was napping so the policeman couldn't ask him.

"'That's nice. Have a good time,' he said as he walked away. My heart still pounding, I thought, *Apparently, he hadn't recognized me as a runaway yet, or worse yet, a murderer.*

"Just then, the announcement came, 'The train leaving for Orlando will be leaving in five minutes.' I jumped up to get in line with Mr. Anderson, just in case the policeman would come nosing back. I also wanted to be able to sit next to my adopted dad on the train.

"When we got on the train, I had my wish. Mr. Anderson was indeed my seat companion. He then introduced himself as Stan. Then he asked my name. "I told him, 'My name is Tiffany Anderson. Isn't that a coincidence we have the same last name?' I was sure thankful that Anderson was such a familiar name.

"He asked me with real concern, 'Where are you heading all by yourself?'

'I'm going to visit my real dad. I haven't seen him for many years since my parents divorced.' I said, that part was true anyway. I was hoping or even pretending that I was really going to see my real dad, or better yet, my brother. Oh, how I missed them.

"I asked, 'Mr. Anderson, are you going to visit your family?'

'You can call me Stan,' he said. He was real quiet for a short time before he answered, his blue eyes showing tears when he did answer, 'Yes, I'm going to see my son. My wife died recently, and I thought a few weeks with my son would help me to be less lonely. My son is a pastor in a small town outside of Orlando.'

"'I'm so sorry to hear about your wife,' I said with concern. Just then, the thought of what I had done earlier raced through my mind. I might have killed a man. Then the saying came back that I had heard in church, 'Jesus loves you, and he will set you free.'

I was suddenly brought back to the present as Mr. Anderson asked, with the same look in his eyes, 'How old are you anyway? I had a daughter that would be about your age. She would be fourteen this year.'

"That's exactly my age, but I couldn't tell him that, so I lied again. 'I'm going to be eighteen soon.' I knew that I could pass for seventeen at least. That way, I wouldn't have to explain why I wasn't in school.

"It was nice talking to Stan, as he was very concerned for me. He continued on, 'Do you have someone to meet you at the train depot when we get to Orlando? If you don't, I can ask my son if he can give you a lift to where you want to go. Are you going to be staying with your father?'

"'I'm going to see how things work out. My father is remarried, and maybe he won't want to bother with me,' I lied partially. I really didn't want to have to lie to Stan. He was being so very nice.

"'Well, if we can be of any help to you any way while I'm in Orlando, please let me know. You can call me at my son's,' he said as he handed me his son's telephone number. I couldn't believe my ears; this man was being so kind. I had never had a man treat me so nice. Later, he even offered to buy some of my meals on the train. He was nothing like the men in my past.

"I thanked him as I accepted the name card and telephone number. I was hoping that I would be able to see him again.

"The trip to Orlando took three days. They were the most pleasurable days of my life. I was so thankful that I had a partner I could talk to. I knew that I couldn't talk to him about my past, but I could tell him about my prospects for the future, even though it was probably only some pipe dream I had. I told him about trying to find my brother. He was interested in everything I had to say. I started to love this man as if he was my real dad. I really wished that he were.

"When we arrived in Florida, I was saddened when we had to part. When he offered again to drive me to my dad's place, I lied again when I told him, 'My dad will meet me at the local hotel he registered me into. Maybe we can meet another time, before you go back to Pennsylvania. I'll call you. Thanks so very much for everything.' I said with sadness as I gave him a peck on his cheek. He then hugged me like I always imagined a real dad would."

Paul gulped but kept quiet. *I wonder if this Mr. Anderson could be our dad.* He thought he better check it out before saying anything to Tiffany.

Chapter 9

Alone in Orlando

Tiffany continued, "After Stan left, I sat in the lonely train depot, not knowing what I was going to do or where I was going to go. I got up and went to the phones and decided to call the cheapest hotel I could find. I had some money but wasn't sure if I could get a job right away.

"As I waited for the cab that was coming to take me to the hotel, I glanced down at a newspaper. I shook my head and looked again. There in bold letters, it read, HAVE YOU SEEN THIS PERSON? Along with this capture was a picture of me when I was eight years old. I was thankful it was the last picture that they had of me. I at least looked much older than the picture. Then as I read on, a description of me followed.: 'Tiffany Dawn, who has dark brown hair with brown eyes, is five feet five inches in height. She is fourteen years old. Please notify the police department of Pittsburgh, Pennsylvania, immediately if you should see this person. She has been involved in theft and other criminal acts.'

"I grabbed the paper and ducked into the cab as soon as it came. I covered my head and face as best as I could so I would not be recognized. I was thankful for the darkness that surrounded me now. I put a kerchief over my head and partially covered my face as I entered the hotel. The clerk behind the desk could not have cared less who I was. She just sat behind the desk chewing her gum. She took my money for the night and told me, 'I needed to be out by 11 a.m. unless I notify them otherwise.'

"I asked her, 'Do you know if there is a beauty shop close by?'

Without looking up, she pointed down the street. 'There's one about a block down the street to the left.' I sure was thankful that it was close. I knew what I had to do early the next morning. I hurried up to my room and grabbed a shower. I was anxious to see what else the paper wrote about Harry. *He must be alive or how would they know that I had stolen the money.*

"I continued to read on: Tiffany is a runaway from her home after attacking her stepfather and stealing money from his billfold. Her parents are very concerned of her whereabouts.

"*Yeah, right!* I said to myself with anger. *Harry just wants to get even with me for getting the best of him. He will never give up on looking for me now. I am really going to have to do a makeover and change my whole appearance. Now I have to worry about two men getting me.*

"As I looked in the mirror and saw my beautiful long dark hair, I knew that I would have to cut my hair and maybe even make it a different color. I wondered what I would look like as a blond. *Tomorrow I'll find out* were my thoughts as I crawled into bed.

"All night, I dreamt about men chasing me all over the country. They were always trying to catch me and hurt me. Then, I would see Stan with a young man looking just like him coming to my rescue.

"The next morning, I wiggled out of bed, confused to where I was at first, then it hit me, I had to change my looks and buy some different clothes right away. I checked the directory and called the beauty shop and made my appointment to get in as soon as possible. The girl told me I could come in at 10 a.m. That was good. *I can stop by on my way to the beauty shop and pick up some different clothes at the little dress shop I noticed last night as the cab drove to the hotel.*

"I quickly fixed my hair differently and put a lot of makeup on so no one would recognize me. I called the hotel desk clerk and told her I was checking out. I would leave the hotel key in the room. I didn't want to take the chance of anyone recognizing me before I exchanged into the new me. Before I realized it, the time read 8:30 a m. I had to get going so I wouldn't miss my appointment. I rushed out and ran across the street and down the block to the dress shop.

"I picked out two pairs of jeans and shirts and a nice pantsuit with a couple of matching tops. I wanted some matching outfits so I could look for work without having to go to a laundry too often. When I paid the clerk, I realized that I had better find a job as soon as possible or I'd be out of money. I had to save some for the beauty shop and room and board, in case I couldn't get work soon.

"I asked the clerk, 'Could I leave my clothes and bag here while I go to an appointment that I have? I'll pick it up in a few hours.'

"The clerk said, 'That will be just fine, I'll probably be off duty then, but I'll tell the next clerk. Just write your name on the package.' I wrote Tiffany Anderson, as I planned to use this name for a long time. *This was good. Now I could go to my appointment and maybe look around for a place to live without dragging my backpack around. I would have until at least 8 p.m. when they closed.*

"I arrived at the beauty shop just in time for my appointment. I didn't want to wait around long to attract attention to myself. On the way, I grabbed a sandwich and Pepsi so I could get going on finding a place to stay as soon as I was through with my changeover.

"I said to the hairdresser, 'I want a complete makeover – haircut, color, and style. I have an important job interview,' I lied again. I couldn't believe all the lies I was telling, and then I remembered: *the truth would set you free.* I quickly said, as an afterthought, 'I was hoping for an interview for a job.'

"'What kind of work are you looking for?' Sue, the hairdresser, asked with concern.

"'I'm looking for anything, but hoping to get into waitress work or whatever is out there. I am also looking for a place to live near my job, as I don't have a car.' I figured that waitress work was the one thing I knew how to do, as I had to do that for so many years while living with my family. Suddenly, I had a pang of guilt run over me. *I hope that Mom is okay. I hope Harry will not take it out on her what I did to him.*

"My thoughts were interrupted as I heard, 'Hey, you're in luck!' Sue said with enthusiasm. 'I am looking for a roommate as we speak. I live just a few blocks from here. I also heard that they are hiring waitresses at the Cafe Delos up the street. It's a real nice classy restaurant, and the pay and tips aren't half-bad. You have to be eighteen to apply, but you're eighteen, aren't you?'

"I nodded in response; she took that for a yes. She continued, 'In fact, when we get done with you, you will, for sure, look eighteen. Then we'll go over there and I'll introduce you to the boss. He's a real good friend of mine.'

"'Why would you do that for me, a perfect stranger? You don't know anything about me,' I said.

"'Oh,' she said, 'I could see that you are okay in my book. I'll call my friend, while you sit under the dryer, and see if he will meet us at the restaurant when we finish here. I will be able to take off for the day and maybe we can get you settled.'

"When Sue came back, she said, 'That was fine, my friend will be glad to give you an interview.'

"We chatted on until we were finished with my makeover. I looked in the mirror, and I didn't even recognize myself. As a blond, I looked pretty good. 'Oh, I feel so much better,' I exclaimed. 'Thanks so much.' I paid the receptionist and gave Sue a big tip. As we walked out of the salon, I knew that I had found a true friend.

"She took me over to the restaurant and introduced me to Bill, her friend. He was a very likable fellow and handsome also. Immediately, I liked him. I could tell by his sparkling blue eyes that he was a good and honest man. I hadn't known many of those. This was a new feeling for me, as I hated men for so long.

"My train of thought was broken just then as Bill said, 'You've got the job as waitress here whenever you can start. You'll be starting at $3.50 per hour, with tips. We will furnish the uniforms. If you want, I will pay you in cash until you get settled so you won't have to worry about taxes right away. You will have to bring a social security card or an identification card with your age and address after you get settled. I understand that you will be staying with Sue.'

"'Oh yes,' I said. 'If she still would like me to.'

"'It's as good as done. You can pay me half the rent and half the utilities, which would be about $150 per month, as soon as you're able to start paying. Remember you're doing me a favor also.' Sue continued, 'As soon as you are ready, I'll show you where I live, and you can bring your belongings over and move in now, if you want.'

"'Oh, that would be wonderful. I only have a couple of bags. I travel light. I left them at the shop a block away. I'll get them, and you can show me your place when I get back. It'll only be a minute, if you want to wait here,' I said with happiness.

"I was elated; today was going so well I couldn't believe it. I had a place to live and a job both at once. I guess there are people that are good. I have met a few already. I was so happy; I couldn't help but say, 'Thank you, Jesus.'

"The next morning, I took a bus downtown to the place that Bill sent me to pick up a Florida name card with my new address and name on it. I felt that I finally was my own person."

"I'm so grateful that God sent all these people to help you get through all of this," Paul said.

Tiffany looked at her brother with a new insight as she continued on with her story.

Chapter 10

Tiffany's First Job

"I started working that next Monday morning. I loved my new job and all the people around me. I especially enjoyed living with Sue. She and Bill were so very nice to me.

"I was so happy that I decided to call Stan to let him know about my good fortune. I called the number of his son that he had given me.

"'Hi, Stan, this is Tiffany. Do you remember me from the train? I just wanted to let you know that I have a new address and telephone number. I'm fine and have a job and am staying with a very good friend I met.' I gave him my number.

"Stan was excited. 'I am so happy to hear from you. I was hoping that you would call before I left to return to Pittsburgh. I will call you when I come through here again. I have your new number. If anything happens, anything at all, please, call my son. Thank you so very much for calling me. I will hope to see you next time I come back,' Stan continued.

"Shortly after I had been working for about two months, Sue and Bill introduced me to their friend Jim. He was the first date I had ever had. I really liked him. He had blond hair and beautiful blue eyes, which had the same sparkle that Bill's had. I knew right away that we would be great friends. He worked at a nearby shop and was going to college. He was nineteen, but I couldn't tell him that I was only fourteen. I was going to turn fifteen in a few months; I would tell him then. We had lots of fun together when we all went together as a group.

"I had been working for about six months. Life was really great. I was in seventh heaven. I couldn't be happier. Then the bombshell dropped. Bill called me into his office one day and asked, 'I hate to ask you this, but I need to know what your real name is. I have information that you are using a different name. I also heard that you are much younger than eighteen. I want to help you, I just need to know – are you in some kind of trouble?'

"I was frightened now, *What if he had heard about my stepfather and what I had done.* I finally blurted out why I had to lie, 'I needed a job immediately. I had run away from my home in Pittsburgh. I am really almost fifteen years old. Please don't tell anyone about me. I have people who want to hurt me if they find me.' I started crying. I was afraid that Bill would have to report me to the police. 'How did you find out about me?' I had to ask.

"Bill said with kindness, 'Sue saw your picture in the paper and put two and two together. We wanted to make sure you were that girl before we told you that we knew. We will keep your little secret, and I will tell anyone looking for you that I have not seen any fourteen-year-old girl matching the description in the paper. You can keep your job here. We will be here to help you if you need anything, or if you want us to call your parents, we can do that for you. They are probably very worried about you, or is there anyone else you want us to call?'

"Tears were running down my face as I ran over to Bill. Hugging him, I said, 'Thank you so much, I will make this up to you. Yes, there is someone you can call for me. His name is

Stan Anderson; he lives in Pittsburgh. He knows me, and he will be able to find my mother, but I do not want her to know where I am right now. Her husband is one of the people who want me to come back. I did something to him, and he wants to punish me.'

"Bill was so shocked when I explained some of what happened, but I still was not able to tell him the whole story. I felt confident that he would help me get out of trouble. 'Thank you, Jesus, I am really glad to get that off my chest.' I said without knowing I had said it, but I meant every word of the prayer."

Chapter II

Mom's Tragic Death

"It was almost a year, and I was still working at Cafe Delos. I thought things had finally settled down when Bill called me into his office again. My first reaction was, 'Now what?' I said out loud to no one in particular.

"I was a little apprehensive until I realized Stan was calling. He may have some good news, I hope.

"'This is Tiffany Anderson,' I answered into the phone. 'How are you? It is really good to hear from you. I hope everything is okay.' When I heard a nervous cough on the other end of the line, I just knew that this was not good. 'What is it? Do you have some bad news for me?'

"'I'm in Orlando, at the airport right now. Is there a chance that I can meet with you? I need to speak with you. I have something to tell you that I can't tell you over the phone. When can I meet with you?' He sounded apprehensive and troubled.

"'I'm at the Cafe Delos on Airport Street only a few blocks from the train depot. I can meet you here. I'll be off duty in a few minutes. I'll wait here at a booth near the front door. I'll look for you and wave when you come in. You may not recognize me.'

"I wondered as I hung up, *does he know the truth? Is he coming here to take me back home to go to jail? He wouldn't do that; he has been such a friend. He maybe isn't as nice as you think,* an evil thought crept into my head. I was thankful that I wasn't able to think too long. Before I realized it, Stan walked into the front door. I waved to him.

"As Stan walked over to me, he asked, 'Is this really you, Tiffany?'

"'Yes, do you like the new me?' I answered, somewhat worried what he had to say.

"'You look wonderful, I wouldn't have recognized you. I'm so glad I didn't recognize you,' Stan said with a friendly look in his eyes. I knew then that he really did not come to harm me.

"'What do you mean?' I asked with curiosity.

"'Well,' he started, 'I know who you are. I saw your picture in the paper, and I thought that you might possibly be that person. I was suspicious, so I checked around to see what kind of trouble you were in. Then things were confirmed when I got the call from Bill saying that you wanted me to find your mom.'

"My heart sank as I said quietly, 'Did you come to take me back to go to jail?'

"'No, I just came to help you. Apparently, this fellow that you hit over the head was okay, but he had filed battery charges against you. There was a warrant out for your arrest.

"'Then your mother came forward and told the police about all the things that he had done to you, and with the school reports of your bruises, they were able to put him in jail for abuse. He will be in jail for a couple of years, but when he went to jail, he vowed to get even with you and your mother.'

"'We should be safe for a while anyway, won't we?' I asked with some hope and deep concern for my mom.

"'There's more, I can hardly get myself to tell you this,' Stan said, coming over to me. He sat beside me and giving me a hug, he continued, 'Your mom was found dead in her house last night. It appeared to look like suicide, but the police suspect foul play. Since Harry was sent to jail a few days ago and Frank had just gotten out, they suspect that he may have had something to do with it.'

"Stan held me as my head whirled, and I suddenly felt as if I was going to pass out. "Oh, no, what have I done? I should have never left her alone with those dreadful men. If there were a god, why would he let this happen? How can I believe in someone who does this kind of thing? Now I don't have anyone." I covered my face and started sobbing uncontrollably.

"'You have your friends and me; we will be your family now. Just lean on us and we will help you get through this. None of this is your fault. God did not cause your mom to die. She lived a lifestyle that would eventually turn tragic. I for one am glad that you got away from that situation. You could not have saved your mother from these men. We can just hope and pray that she found the truth and it set her free before she died,' Stan said as he held me, his newfound 'daughter.'

"Still sobbing, I asked, 'what truth are you talking about? This truth keeps avoiding us. I keep having so much fear and trouble. It just keeps getting worse instead of better. When I finally feel things are going good, something bad happens to people around me. Why Mom? I was just starting to understand her and feel better about her. Why can't things just go well? What do I have to do to stop this nightmare? How did Frank get out of jail so fast in the first place? I just wish he would die. Maybe some of this would go away. My mother was weak, but she didn't deserve to die.'

"'No, she certainly didn't deserve that. When your mother realized that you were abused because of the lifestyle she led, she was unable to accept that fact, but she has made it right for you now. Only we will have to go back there and arrange for her funeral and maybe talk with the police to see if we can get some protection for you from Frank.' Stan continued with deep sincerity. And with his arms around me for comfort, I knew that he meant it.

"Noticing me crying, Bill ran over to us and asked with deep concern, 'What is going on here? Are you okay, Tiffany? Is this man hurting you?'

"Stan then explained to Bill all the things that he had related to me. They were both so concerned I knew that they would be there for me and that I could depend on them. They had to be my family now.

"'You certainly can't blame yourself because of your mom's death. When a person lives the way it sounds like she did most of her life, it usually ends tragically. You aren't to blame for any of these things,' Bill also assured me.

"'If you want, you can go back with me on the next plane and get this all settled. We will have to make arrangements for your mother's funeral. I'll be there for you in any way that I can. You think about this and make arrangements for time off work. I will make sure nothing happens to you,' Stan said with the same sincerity.

"I didn't know what to say; all I could think of to say was, 'Why are you doing all of this for me? Why are you being so good to me when you know how many bad things I have done?' I sobbed.

"'You certainly aren't bad. I just knew in my heart that you needed help when I first heard you use my name as yours at the train depot." Stan laughed.

"'Oh no, you mean you figured it out already then? How I had lied to you? And you accepted it and didn't let on!" I said with amusement and puzzlement.

"'I couldn't let on until I knew the whole story. I know the story now; I think I can help you. You check with Bill here about getting off work, and I'll check on a plane ticket for you to come back with me to Pittsburgh,' he said with another hug, which I was really starting to enjoy.

"'You are like a father to me, you have been so kind. Thank you so very much for all you have done for me,' I said as I gave Stan a peck on the cheek before I realized what I was doing.

"Stan was pleased for the kiss on his cheek as he said, 'Yes, you are just like a daughter also. I never got to know my own daughter, but I would like her to be just like you,' he said with the sweetest smile and twinkle in his eyes that I was really beginning to love.

"'You better ask your boss now if you can get off.' Bill was standing beside us and had heard every word Stan had said. I was relieved that I wouldn't have to relate the horrible mess all over again.

"I looked over to Bill, and he saw the question in my eyes and said, 'I see no problem with you having off. I'm sure that we will be able to manage for a little while. Take the time you need, but don't forget to come back. We'll miss you.'

"Bill was very understanding as he heard my dilemma. 'We'll have your job here for you when you get back. Just give us a call when you are ready to come back to work.'

"'What's going on?' Jim happened to walk in just at that time. 'What is all the time off for?' He looked at Bill and back to me with concern. 'Are you leaving us?' he then directed his question to me.

"'Yes, I have to go back home for a while. My mother has passed away," I said, with tears continuing to roll down my face.

"'Oh, I'm so sorry. Is there anything I can do for you? Will you be gone long?' he said with great concern, then he continued sheepishly, 'I'm going to really miss you.' Then he gave me a little peck on my cheek.

"I could feel myself blushing, I turned my face away as I said, 'Thank you all so much for caring. I have to go now, have to pack, and then we are leaving on the first plane back to Pittsburgh. I will miss you all very much,' I said as I ventured a quick smile over to Jim. I thought that I could see a wink as his eyes showed love and concern for me at this time.

"Stan was leaving for the airport then to make the arrangements and said to me, 'You get your bags, and I'll pick you up at your apartment in one hour.'

"'Thanks for all your concern also.' He directed this statement to the others. 'I'll keep her safe and hope she will be back here in a short time.'

"I went to my apartment, packed some clothes in Annie's backpack. I quickly jotted off a note to Sue telling her of the circumstances why I had to leave and that I would call her when I planned on coming back.

"I had real bad feelings about going back. I hated my mother's house and all the memories in it. I was scared that I might run into Frank. I couldn't possibly be more afraid of him as I was right now. I just knew he had something to do with Mom's death. I was so thankful Stan was close by.

"'I really think Frank did kill Mom. Oh, poor Mom, I really did love her. Even she didn't know that. I'm so sorry,' I said to Stan through the tears as we sat in the airplane.

"Stan understood, as he said, 'Things will be okay, I'm going to be with you all the time that I can. The police are looking for Frank, and he may be in custody as we speak. They understand the circumstances.'

"When we arrived back in Pittsburgh and went to my old house, Stan stayed with me. Tears were always close to the surface, but I knew that I had to get things taken care of before I really fell apart. I wasn't in any mood for any more surprise. I was so thankful to have Stan there for me. I really appreciated him, as I knew that I couldn't handle everything alone.

"I packed all of Harry's things up and put them in a box and sent them to the prison where he was. I put a note in it saying, 'Mrs. Dawn is gone now, and we have to get rid of the house.' I signed it anonymous. The rest of our things we packed up and put them into boxes. I called Anne's church to see if they could use the articles and come and pick them up. They could do with them as they wished. I knew that Mom had many nice and expensive gifts that she had gotten from her old boyfriends, but I did not want anything to do with any of these things. I felt that they were dirty. I then called the rental agency where we had rented the furniture to come and get them as soon as possible. I did not want to have to deal with anything after the funeral.

"Stan went with me to the funeral home and helped me make plans for the funeral for 10 a.m. the following morning. As we walked into the funeral home after hearing how terrible she had died, I knew that I could not see Mom. I wanted to remember her as she was before I left, so I decided to have a closed casket. She had been so very concerned for me the last time I saw her. I was hoping I could try to get a hold of my brother to see if he could come to the funeral, but I had no idea where to find him. In fact, I didn't even know my real name, much less his. I was just grateful that Stan was there, even though he wasn't family; I pretended that he was my dad.

"When Stan had to leave to go back to work, he said, 'I really hate to leave you. Are you sure you will be okay tonight? I will see you at the funeral tomorrow, as I have to get back to work now.'

"'Stan, I really do appreciate all the things you have done. I'll be okay; I'm going over to my friend Annie's house and will stay with them tonight. I love you for all you have done. I'll see you tomorrow at the funeral. Thanks again,' I said with appreciation and then gave him a little peck on the cheek. Which, afterward, I noticed his eyes twinkling again.

"After Stan left, I went over to my friend Annie's house. I really wanted to see her, as it had been a long time since I'd seen her.

"When I arrived, happy to see me, Annie said, 'We have been very concerned about you and your mother. Your mother had come here a week ago and was worried about a man named Frank. She said she was frightened for herself and for your life. We prayed with her, and she accepted the Lord. She felt more at peace after our prayer. She asked me to give you this letter if something happened to her. The next week, they said she had committed suicide. I don't believe that for one minute. She was very frightened. I'm so sorry." Annie hugged me as she gave me the letter.

"Opening the letter, tears came down my face. It was hard lately not to be crying.

This was what the letter said:

> This letter is to my dear Tiffany. I hope that I may be able to see you before you get this letter, but if I don't, remember I love you. I am so sorry for all I have put you through. I never thought that Harry would also do the things that Frank did to you and hurt you like they both did. I know the truth now, and I can't handle this anymore. I have notified the police and told them about everything, and they said that you would be set free of any wrongdoing. But watch out for Harry when he gets out of jail in about two years. But my biggest concern for you is that Frank may hurt you. He is out of prison now, and I have seen him around. He is stalking me, and I'm not afraid if he hurts me. I have God in my life now, but that Frank may come after you. I have written a letter that I have hidden in the black box in our secret place. I want you to get what's in the box and take the letter and give it to a man named Stan Anderson at the FBI. He is really more than a friend, but I can't explain that to you at this time. I know that I have not been a real good mom to you, but I have changed, and now that I know the truth, it has set me free. I pray that you will also find this truth, and it will also set you free. If something should happen to me, I want you to find your brother and your real dad. Stan will help you with this. I love you very much, and may God keep you safe and happy. Someday I know that I may see you in the life hereafter with God. Love forever, Mom.

"I always kept that letter, as it was the only time that my mom told me she really loved me. I was so glad that I could read these words. I wish she could have said them to me in person, but now she is gone forever. She said something about seeing me in 'life hereafter'; whatever did she mean? This was becoming another mystery.

"I then remembered the hiding space where Mom had told me to look for the letter for Stan. I knew that I had to get the letter before the house was closed. I had forgotten about the little box when I had packed everything up. I hoped that it was still there.

"I quickly told Annie, 'I have to go back to the house, I forgot something that I had to get. I will be back as soon as possible and we will talk. Tell your mom I really appreciate her letting me stay tonight. I know that I could not stay in the house tonight or any night. It is really spooky there.

"I ran back to the house and found the little black box just where it was supposed to be. Inside the box was a picture of my brother Paul and a small package. Inside the package was Mom's wedding ring with a note wrapped around it that read:

> This is the ring that I got from your real dad, whom I loved more than anyone. Please keep it, and someday, maybe you will find him and your brother. Here is the last picture I have of your brother. I want you to have it now. I have treasured his memory all of these years. The letter, which is with this, is sealed, and I want you to give it to Stan Anderson. Do not let anyone else see or read it. This is a very important paper that will help convict Frank, and maybe he will finally stay in jail so you will not have to worry about him anymore. I am being followed all the time, so I cannot get this to where it needs to go. I will depend on you to do this, my darling daughter. With all of my love, Mom.

"This was really freaking me out now. I was sure glad that I was able to stay at Annie's house. Things were just too weird around here. *I will come back tomorrow after the service and get everything finished here and never have to see this place again.* I grabbed my clothes for the funeral and my box, placed it safely in my bag, and hurried out the door before it got too dark. If Frank had been watching Mom, he may be out there someplace and watching me. I ran faster as I thought about that possibility. I then decided that I would sneak around the back way in case Frank was watching the house so he would not know that I was over at Annie's. I certainly didn't want them to get hurt.

"When I finally got to Annie's after the long way around sneaking behind things, she asked me as I came in huffing and puffing, 'Is everything all right? You seem very nervous and upset.'

"'I guess I'm just a little concerned about what you said about Mom. That maybe she was hurt by this guy named Frank. I just don't want you to get hurt, so I took a different way here so if he were watching our house, he wouldn't see me come here,' I said with fear.

"The next morning, at the funeral, I sat with Stan so no one would know that I was even there. Annie and her mom and dad sat behind me. I was so thankful that they came. There were very few people there. We had moved so many times that Mom never got involved with too many people, only those dreadful men Frank used to bring home with him. I just dared any of them to come. All of a sudden, I thought that I saw Frank out of the corner of my eyes. I didn't want to make a scene, as I didn't think that he could recognize me. I gave Stan a little nudge and nodded my head toward where I thought I had seen Frank. When Stan looked, Frank had disappeared. I was afraid now that he may try something.

For the service lasted only a short time. When it was over, they took my mother in the hearse, and we followed out to the burial grounds. As Mom was lowered into the ground, I had a funny feeling that someone was watching every thing that was going on. I was glad to get out of there. We did not plan lunch, so most of the people left to go home from there.

"Stan took Annie, her folks, and me out to eat. We went to an out-of-place restaurant so if Frank were around, he wouldn't know where we went. I was happy for that. I wasn't anxious to have to go back to the house and finish the packing anyway.

"After lunch, Stan took me back to the house and stayed with me as long as he could. When he had to leave, he said, 'Call me when you finish here, and I will take you to the airport to catch your flight back to Orlando, which I have arranged for tonight at 10 p.m.' I was glad he made the flight for that early, as I didn't want to stay any longer, than I had to, especially as long as Frank was out there somewhere.

"I had just finished settling everything and the last box had left the house when I heard the door open. At first I thought it was probably Annie running over to visit. As I turned around, I gasped with fright, 'What are you doing here? Get out!' I screamed at Frank as he came toward me.

'I backed slowly to the stairway and quickly ran upstairs and barricaded my door, which I knew how to do very well. He followed me upstairs and tried yanking on my door to get it open. I was so frightened; I prayed, 'Please don't let him get in here.'

"I could hear him swearing outside my door when he couldn't get in to my room. He finally went to my mom's room, where I could hear him rummaging around. I grabbed my things, put them in Annie's backpack, and slipped out the window and slithered down the tree, which I had done so many times before. I ran as fast as I could to Annie's house, to the back door, and knocked.

"'Please, please be here,' I prayed as it took a little while before they answered.

"Annie's mom came to the door and quickly let me in. She could tell that I was scared and asked, 'What's wrong? You look like someone is after you. Are you hurt or anything?'

"I rambled on as I said, 'Frank came to the house just now; he is rummaging around in everything that is left. I think he is looking for the letter that my mom wrote and said to give to the police. Please, I need to call the police and tell them that someone is burglarizing my house and maybe they can catch him this time.'

"Annie's dad quickly called the police, and later, I called Stan to tell him to meet me behind an old building near the school. I gave him the address and said my last goodbyes and told Annie that I needed her backpack just a little longer as I hurried out the back door.

"Just as I got on the street, I could see Frank's car drive out of the driveway coming right toward me. I slipped behind a bush and prayed that he did not see me. He quickly sped past as we could hear the screaming of the police cars coming, as they screeched to a stop at our house. It looked like Frank had gotten away again. I couldn't believe it! He was so slippery. *The rat!*

"I got up quickly and ran on to where I was to meet Stan. He came immediately, and we sped off to the airport. During the drive, I handed the little black box to Stan and said, 'I think this letter is what Frank is after; Mom left a note and said I was supposed to give it to you. In another letter, she says that it has some evidence that will help Frank go to jail and maybe stay there.'

"Stan thanked me, took the letter, and placed it in his pocket. He then noticed the ring in the box; tears suddenly came to his eyes. 'Where did you get this ring?' he asked.

"'It was my mom's; she said she got it from my dad, the only man she ever loved.' I asked, 'Why, do you recognize it from somewhere?'

"'I guess it just looked like one I had given to someone so very long ago.' He didn't say anything more about the ring but was real quiet until we got to the airport.

"When we arrived at the airport, Stan went with me to the plane to make sure that I got on and that Frank wasn't lurking around. Frank seemed to have a bad habit of doing that lately.

"I hated to be leaving Stan, but I was just glad to be getting back to Orlando and my friends. This had been a trying time for me. I never wanted to go through this again.

"The wait was not too long. I was glad, and so was Stan; we stayed in crowds so no one would find us easily. When the plane came and I was ready to board, I gave Stan a big hug and a big kiss on the cheek this time and said, 'Thank you for all that you have done, and I'll never forget you. I love you.'

"Stan gave me the biggest hug and gave me a kiss on my forehead, which took me by surprise, but I enjoyed it, as he said, 'You take care of yourself now, and I'll get a hold of you as soon as I can. I love you too." As I walked down the ramp to the plane, I could see tears on his face through my own tears. I really loved that man."

Paul listened, and what Tiffany had said confirmed his suspicion that Stan was more to them than Tiffany had known, but he had to be certain.

Chapter 12

Another Escape

"At last I was on my way hoping to get back to some normalcy. I laid my head back, thinking about all the things that Stan had done for me. He really was like a father, which I imagined one would be like. I fell sound asleep. This was the first real sleep that I had since I had left Orlando oh so long before.

"I was suddenly awakened by a nudge on my shoulder; 'Are you Tiffany Anderson?' the voice of the stewardess startled me.

"'Why, what's going on? Where are we?' I stammered as I awoke from the long hard sleep.

"'You have a phone call. We have landed in Orlando. Follow me, I will show you where the phone is while the others passengers are getting off.'

"I staggered up, followed the stewardess, and thought, *Who can this be? Stan is the only one who knows that I'm on this flight, I hope anyway.* I answered the phone cautiously, 'This is Tiffany.' I didn't want to say too much in case it was Frank.

"'Tiffany, this is Stan. I had to get a hold of you before you got off the plane. You must stay on the plane and not get off in Orlando. Frank has eluded the police again, and he was last seen on his way to Orlando. He may be waiting for you somewhere in the airport in Orlando. I have made arrangements for you to go on to Miami and stay at the Day's Inn near the airport. I will contact you when you get there. I have to go now, but please do exactly as you are told for your safety. I have contacted Bill, and he knows that you will not be to work for now. Please take care, God be with you, and soon the truth will set you free. I'll talk with you later.'

"As I replaced the phone, I wondered again why Stan was being so helpful and worried about me. I slipped back to my seat and pulled out the little black box that had Mom's ring in it and remembered what Stan had said when he had first seen the ring. 'He had given one to someone special years ago, just like it.' *Could that have been my mother? He did say he had a daughter just the same age as me. Maybe* . . . My thoughts trailed off as passengers started coming on the plane. I remembered Stan's call and quickly placed the box back in my backpack, sunk down in my seat, and hid myself behind a book. I was thankful that a large robust man sat next to me to outshadow me.

"I had to think of what I was going to do now because I had to find another job. Things just kept getting more complicated. Then I remembered the words Stan said, 'God will take care of you, and the truth will set you free.' I have to find out the truth pretty soon or all of this will drive me nuts. When the plane landed in Miami, it was about 3 a.m. It was eerie, but I was glad that it was dark so no one could recognize me again.

"I hurried to get a cab and on to the Day's Inn as directed. I registered and went directly to my room, threw my backpack down, and fell on the bed. I fell sound asleep and didn't awaken until the ringing of the phone startled me. When I first awoke, I couldn't remember where I was. I looked at the clock and noticed that it was 8 a.m. When I got my senses back, I said to myself, *That has to be Stan.*

"'Hello, this is Tiffany,' I said, hopeful that it was Stan. I had a lot of questions for him.

"'Tiffany, this is Stan. I'm glad that you made it there okay. I have the room for you for one week. That will give you some time to get a job and get another place later. I have sent money to you by Western Union, and you can pick it up in the hotel lobby. If you have a chance, try to change your looks so you won't be recognized if anyone does come down that way. The police are looking for Frank in Florida, so hopefully we can get him. They have the letter that you gave to me, and they have a warrant out for his arrest for your mother's death. He has so many people in areas of high places that help him that we are having a hard time locating him. I think you will be safe; just be on your guard.'

"'Why are you doing all of this for me?' I finally had to ask. 'Are you involved with the police?'

"'I may as well tell you; I'm working undercover for the FBI. That's why I had to be so secretive. I won't be able to contact you again for a while, but if you have any trouble, please call my son, the card I gave you, and he will be able to help you. God be with you, and I pray you will be okay,' Stan said with reassurance. I always felt better when I could talk with Stan for some reason.

"After talking with Stan, I realized how hungry I was. I hadn't eaten since I had that little snack on the plane coming from Pittsburgh. That had to be over twelve hours ago. I looked in the mirror, and remembering Stan's words, I quickly got my scissors out and trimmed my hair. It had grown so much that most of my auburn hair had returned so it could easily be dark again without too much trouble. The last time Frank saw me was when I was blond, so this should be a change. I quickly showered, and after dressing, I hurried downstairs to check on the money Stan said he had sent. Sure enough, there was $200, which would help me along until I could get a job.

"They had a nice restaurant at the hotel. I got a booth and ordered a big breakfast. I didn't know when I would be eating again. I grabbed a paper and started to look for jobs in the want ads.

"After eating, I checked a few jobs around the area that I noticed in the paper. The jobs were hard to get as the minorities, who worked the jobs for lesser pay, filled them most.

"I was starting to feel defeated after looking for a whole week. I knew that I had to find something soon as my money was running out, and I only had one day left at the hotel. Then that day, I finally noticed an ad in the paper for a waitress at a restaurant and bar called the Hole in the Wall.

"When I walked into the dingy bar, I could see that it wasn't a very nice place. But my being desperate for a job, I applied, and with my experience, I was hired right away. They didn't even ask how old I was. I told them I didn't have a permanent address yet, but they accepted me anyway. They paid me $2 per hour, with tips. Uniforms were also furnished. They were nothing like the uniforms I had at the last place. These were so skimpy that I felt like I was wearing nothing. I didn't like the idea, but it was a job. I figured this would help until I could get something better.

"I started working the very next day. I had enough money to pay for a small boarding room, which I paid weekly. It was a dump in the poorer part of town, but I guess I was poor like the rest. My boss was a grumpy man with bulging eyes that never seemed to look happy. His eyes matched his bulging belly. When he talked, he bellowed with a thick European accent. He was tough on his workers. We had to be working all the time. He would not allow us to chat between each other or even the customers. I hated this, as I never had a chance to have any friends. The customers were usually rough – and tough-looking men who would get drunk and paw on the waitresses. I hated this. I had sworn so many years ago that I wouldn't allow men to do that to me again. But this was my food and water.

"Then one day, I noticed a clean, well-dressed middle-aged man come into the restaurant. I had seen this fellow come in a few times before. This time, he came over and sat in my area. When I asked him, what I could do for him, I couldn't believe the answer he gave.

"'You are such a pretty girl, what are you doing in a dump like this?' he asked.

"I was stunned; the other men in this place didn't treat me at all like this, and I was flattered as I said, 'I'm working here just until I can find something better.'

"'Maybe you could help me. I have a great offer for you,' he said with the sweetest smile.

"I was leery, as I had heard the other girls tell of the pimps that would come in and try to get the girls to come and work for them. 'If you came in here to get me to be a lady of the night, you better think twice because I would never do that,' I said with more confidence than I thought I had.

"'I should hope not. That is nothing like what I had in mind. My name is Tom Belie; I have a modeling place downtown where we model clothes for the local dress shops. We could sure use a beautiful girl like you as a model at our shop,' he said with eyes that sparkled.

"I was taken aback somewhat; he wanted me to be a model, and I couldn't believe what I was hearing. I stammered and said, 'I would certainly have to think about this.' Just then, my boss came over and said in his usual voice, 'I told you I don't want you chatting with the customers. Just do your job!'

"'I will order a cup of coffee and a hamburger to get him off your back,' he said with a wink.

"When I came back with the coffee, he handed me a card and said, 'Here is my card, you take it and check us out if you want to. I will come back in a few days, and you can give me your answer then. I think you will be glad to be able to get away from this joint.'

"I just smiled and said, 'I'll check things out and talk to you when you come back. Thank you.'

"Later after I was off work, I asked my co-workers about this fellow. May, one of the other waitresses, said, 'Oh, that man is a big shot down at the model place. They model for the local dress shops. I sure wouldn't mind if he would ask me for a job. I'd leave here in a minute.'

"The next day was my day off, so I decided to do a little checking on my own. I talked to a lady named Sandy at the shop, and she raved up and down about Tom. 'He is the nicest man to work for. If you work here you would just love it like we do.'

"That night, I was so excited that I called Sue, my old roommate, and said, 'Hi, Sue, this is Tiffany. How are you, Bill, and Jim?'

"'Sue said, 'Oh, Tiffany, I'm so happy to hear from you. I heard about your situation and hope you are okay. Bill says hi, and Jim calls every day to see if you have come back yet. He sure misses you like we all do. Where are you and what have you been up to?'

"'I have been working at this bar called Hole in the Wall, a dump, but I think I am going to start a modeling job for a fellow I met. I'm so excited I had to call you.'

"'Be careful about those places; they sometimes lure girls into them and make you into prostitutes. You certainly don't want to get involved with that,' Sue cautioned me.

"'I checked everything out, and it is all on the up and up. I even talked to one of the girls who work at the place, and they all just love working there. Have to go now, my money is running out. Say hi to everyone for me and also Jim. I will try to call you later when I get more settled. I don't have a permanent address yet,' I said as the operator got on the phone and said, 'Your three minutes are up.'

"I couldn't wait to get to work to see if Tom would show up. He said he would be back in a few days. Maybe he wouldn't show up and was just feeding me a line. I started to have that negative thinking again when I saw him sit down in my area close to the end of my shift. I was glad of that. *Maybe I will get a chance to talk with him without my grumpy boss nosing around.*

"My heart was beating so hard I was afraid it was being heard. As I walked over to Tom's booth, he asked, 'Have you thought anymore about my job offer?'

"Have I thought anymore! – It hasn't been off my mind for three days! I just smiled and was about to give him my answer when the boss trampled over and hovered above me. I didn't dare say anything at this time. I certainly didn't want him to know about this other job right now. He would give me such a hard time. Tom noticed my predicament and quickly changed the subject and ordered a cup of coffee and a donut. As I came back with his order, he asked, 'When do you get off work? Maybe we can talk then.'

"'I'll be done here in about a half hour,' I said with relief that I was almost done.

"'Good, I'll wait for you, and I will take you out to eat in a real restaurant where we will be able to talk,' he said with another sweet smile.

"When I finished cleaning up, I grabbed my backpack, which I kept with me at all times; I never dared to leave it at my rooming house – everything usually got stolen there. I came out, and Tom led me out the front door. We got into his beautiful Buick. I had never been in as nice a car as this. We drove to a fancy restaurant downtown, and Tom asked after we walked in and sat down, 'Would you like to have a drink before we order?'

"'No, I don't drink,' I said, trying to sound as grown-up as I could. I didn't have a valid ID; I certainly wasn't old enough to drink, but I couldn't tell him that. That was one thing I had to get when I got settled, as well as a permanent address, if I took this job.

"My thoughts were broken when Tom asked after the waitress took our order, 'Well, what have you decided to do? Do you think you want the job?'

"'The job sure sounds promising, I have thought a lot about it." That was an understatement. I continued, trying to sound more adultlike. 'What is the pay, and when would you need me?'

"I almost dropped my teeth when he said, 'We would start you at $15 per hour, and we will furnish all the beautician costs. You certainly don't look like you need beauty work, but we do many changes for the modeling. Does that sound fair to you?'

"Fair? – That sound like a robbery! I thought, but I said, 'Oh yes, I think that would be adequate. When would you like me to start, if I did take the job?' I asked, not wanting to appear overanxious.

"'We can go over to the shop right now, and you can look around meet some of the models, there are a few working tonight. Then, if you decide to work for us, we can draw up a contract, and you can start Monday morning. How does that sound?' he said with that beautiful smile.

"We walked over to the plant, which happened to be just across the street from where we were. When I walked in, I couldn't believe how luxurious everything looked. I couldn't wait to be a part of this. Tom introduced me to some of the models, and then, he introduced me to Sandy, whom I had talked with before. 'This is Sandy; she will be the one who will train you in.' Sandy was just like I pictured her – a beautiful person, with a lovely smile and eyes, which sparkled as she looked over to Tom. I sensed more of a relationship between them than a business relationship. They both seemed like wonderful people.

"'I'm so glad to meet you. You're the one I talked to over the phone,' I said as I handed her my hand.

"She shook my hand and said, 'I will be training you in if you decide to take the job, which I really hope you will. We will love to add you to our little family.'

"Tom then said, "If we are going to get Tiffany into our family, we better get her signed up. We will start you on a contract for six months, and if you like it here, we will continue the contract. How does that sound?'

"'That sounds great, I will be glad to be part of this family,' I said with excitement.

"'That's good. I'll make up the contract, and we'll see you early Monday morning,' he said as he shook my hand with a firm but friendly handshake.

"'Do you have a place to stay near here?' Sandy asked. 'If you don't, I need a roommate, are you interested? If you are, you can come over and I'll show you around and you can move in tonight.'

"'That would be wonderful, I do need a place to live,' I said with gratefulness.

"'It's all settled then. You will be paying two hundred dollars a month plus half the utilities,' she said.

"I went to the phone then and called my old boss and told him, 'You can take your job and shove it. I am not coming back there anymore.' I could hear swearing at the other end as I hung up.

"That very same night, I moved in with Sandy, my backpack and all."

Paul said, "I'm so thankful; it seems that you apparently had God's guardian angels with you all the time."

Chapter 13

From Riches to Rags

"I started working the next Monday morning. Sandy was a gem. She taught me my job. I loved working with her and Tom. The others were always very friendly and helpful also. After about two weeks, Sandy said, 'I have taught you everything that you need to know for this job. You will be on your own starting next Monday. I will be starting my new job a few blocks from here. I'm going to go into acting, which is my first love; I will only be a short ways away.' I hated to see Sandy leave but was very happy for her. I would see her every day, as we roomed together.

"This job turned out to be as nice as the one I had in Orlando. I couldn't believe my good fortune and much more money also. I couldn't get used to the money and had a hard time knowing how to spend it. I decided to try and save as much as I could; I never knew when I might need it.

"I had been working at my new job for six months. It was still an enjoyment every day I would go to work. Even the photographers, who I got to know very well, treated me with much dignity. I really liked that. I was beginning to feel a part of the family.

"Then one day, I walked into the shop. I confronted another fellow in Tom's office. He was robust, had an evil, piercing look in his eyes. He reminded me of Frank. I was scared. I asked with fear, but tried to keep composure, 'Where is Tom this morning?'

"The robust man came over to me and gave me his large ugly hand and said, 'Tom doesn't work in this department anymore. I'm Hank, and you are our property now.'

"'What do you mean?" I stammered. 'I do not belong to anyone, I work for Tom,' I said with defiance.

"Hank came toward me and grabbed for me. Before I could move away from him, he held me and started pawing at me saying in his ugly voice, 'You are some beauty. You will make many a man happy.

"I was angry now. I struggled to get away from him by giving him a shove as I said, 'No man owns me! I will quit this job before I will ever do what you want me to.'

"Tom came in just then and could see what was happening and said, 'Leave Tiffany alone! She is not your property! She works for me.'

"Tom gently pushed me behind him and whispered in my ear, 'Run to the restaurant down the street and wait for me there, I will take care of things here. Now go!"

"He didn't have to tell me twice. I scooted out the door and down the block before he finished his words. I was shaking terribly as I entered the restaurant. I went over to a booth in the back part of the room where I could watch the door inconspicuously. I ordered a cup of coffee. My hands shook as I sipped on my coffee. Suddenly, it hit me. Two days ago, there were different men in the shop taking pictures of the models. It never dawned on me at the time.

"*Oh no,* I suddenly thought, *maybe those pictures got out and maybe Frank or one of his goons might recognized me.* Tom walked in just then and sat across from me. I had to have some answers.

"Tom looked sad and angry as he asked, 'Are you okay? Did Hank hurt you before I got there?'

"'No, I'm okay. A little shaky, but I will be okay. How about you, are you okay? You won't be able to go back there after what just happened.'

"'I told him that I quit also. He was very angry. He said something about suing us. He said that you were under contract to them. All the employers under contract were his property. When I told him that your contract had run out two days earlier, he was so angry. He knew that he had no case against us,' Tom said with some reassurance.

"I had to ask then, 'You remember those men who were in the other day taking photos of the models? Who were those men?'

"'They were probably men from the new owners. They usually sent men over to check out the models and the company when they buy or have a takeover'"

"'You knew about the takeover then?' I asked, feeling some anger against Tom.

"I knew that there was a possibility of it, but I never thought they would move in this fast. I meant to tell everyone about it this morning. That's why I didn't get your contract up-to-date sooner. I wasn't sure that you would want to work for new owners. I'm really sorry that this all happened.' My anger subsided as he explained.

"'Who is the new owner?' I asked, not sure if I wanted to hear.

"'The big name behind the takeover is Frank Papy. He isn't the one that is running the place though,' he said.

"Suddenly, I turned pale and gasped. 'What's wrong? You look like you've seen a ghost.'

"I couldn't breathe, all I could think of was to get away, 'I got to get out of here, right now. Could you take me home?'

"'What's wrong? Do you know this person I talked about?' he asked with worry on his face. He certainly did not want to scare me.

"'I will explain later as we drive. I really have a terrible headache.' I lied just so we could get out of there. Tom laid money on the table for our coffee, and we took off out the door. I was really frightened now, I didn't dare tell Tom all the gory details, and it just might get him into trouble. I just said as we took off, 'Watch out for this Frank guy, he is a gangster; I can't tell you more.' I had such a headache. My head was screaming, 'Get away, away, away now!' The sound was so strong, that I had to hold my head.

"Tom saw how uncomfortable I looked and reached in the back of his car and brought out an old floppy hat. 'Here, put this on. Maybe it will keep the sun out of your eyes. Now you look just like one of us guys. Shall I call you Samuel?' he said with a grin, trying to cheer me up.

"When we arrived at my apartment, Tom reached into his billfold and handed me $400 as he said, 'Here, you may need this before you will be able to get another job.'

"'You don't owe me this much for working,' I said as he gave me the money.

"'Yes, some of this is your severance pay. You keep all of it. You be sure and let us know how you are doing and if you have any trouble. You be sure and call Sandy. Or me,' he said out of concern.

"'Thank you for all you have done. I'll let you know when I get to wherever I will be going. I may have a job in another town,' I said a little white lie so he wouldn't worry about me. I jumped out of the car, waved to him, and quickly ran into my apartment.

"When I got into the apartment, I locked the door. I was getting paranoid now after what I had just heard. I went into the bathroom and looked in the mirror. I knew just what kind of disguise I was going to have this time. Tom had given me the idea, and my new name will be Samuel. I cut most of my hair off, looked in the mirror, and thought, *This time, I am going to be a boy; that way no one will be pawing at me.*

"I noticed a pair of bib overalls that had been at the closet for a long time, and I had never seen Sandy wear them. I grabbed a couple baggy shirts, which was with them. I traded my pantsuit for the pants. I quickly jotted a note and left $200 in an envelope with this explanation, 'I had to go back to Minnesota because of an illness in the family.' They would never check out that rigid cold country. I told her that I had traded my pantsuit for her old bib overalls and two shirts. I hoped that she didn't mind. I quickly put on the bib overalls and noted that I was showing too much on top to be a boy. I looked around to see if I could find something to bind me up some. I found an Ace bandage in the closet, which worked perfectly to hide my expanding top. I put on my bibs, big shirt, floppy hat, and, looking in the mirror, thought, *Now, I am a boy*. My shoes were sneakers, so they fit right in. I placed my money that I had saved and what Tom had given me in the safe place in my backpack along with my picture and valuables. The only clothes I had were what I had on and a couple of jeans I had bought earlier. I darted out the back way and down the street to catch the city bus. I didn't know where I was going to end up, but I knew that I had to get away. Looking back, a tear fell, as I had really loved this place. Then the thought came back, 'God will take care of you, and the truth will soon set you free.'

"As we entered a small town of Miramar, the bus sped by a Greyhound bus station as we continued on toward the open fields and orchards, northwest of Miami. Suddenly a sign loomed ahead, which read: Orange Pickers Needed at the Orange Orchard, Two Miles Ahead.

"I watched for the Orange Orchard, and when the bus stopped in front of a building lined with oranges and other fruits, I could smell the fragrant odor of the fresh fruit, which gnawed at my empty stomach. I got off, grabbed a few oranges, and went into the building. An older man with long beard asked, 'Could I help you, young man?' At first, I didn't realize he was talking to me; I had forgotten for a second that I was a man today.

"I gave the man money for the oranges I had picked up and answered in my lowest man voice, 'I hear you are looking for pickers. I am a very good worker and will be ready to pick anytime you need.'

"'What is your name, and how old are you, and where did you come from?' the man asked.

"'My name is Samuel Anderson. I'm eighteen years old. And I am from Minneapolis, Minnesota.' *I figured that they wouldn't question this.* 'Many people visit from there every winter.'

"'Well, I'll take your word for it, gets mighty cold up there, doesn't it?' He didn't even wait for me to answer, as he continued, 'You probably are a hard worker coming from that part of the country. We will pay you $20 per day, and we pay every day you work. So if you don't show up or it rains, you won't get paid. Sound okay?' I nodded yes, and then he said, 'The truck will be leaving in fifteen minutes.' Noticing my backpack, he continued, 'You can store your bag over in the lockers at the end of the store until you get in at night. You will work from 8 a.m. until 8 p.m., unless it is raining or too cold to go out.'

"'Thank you for giving me a chance; you won't be sorry,' I said as I ran to the back of the store to place my backpack in the locker. I quickly took my valuables out and slipped them in my deepest pocket with the zipper so it wouldn't get lost. I figured I had better use the rest room here. It was hard telling where I would find a place out in the fields.

"I jumped into the back of the big truck and rode out to the orchard with all the other guys. They were all of different nationalities and color. Some didn't even speak English. Somehow, they all knew what to do. *Hey, this wasn't half bad being a fellow,* I thought. At least they weren't pawing on me. That was nice for a change. It was actually fun to be a guy.

"Every day, we would meet and work from 8 a.m. to 8 p.m. The only problem I had was when I would have to use the outside biff when the men would all find a large tree. They would tease me, but I would just say, 'You know I'm from

Minnesota, where it is so cold that if we would go bathroom outside, we would freeze everything off, so we all get in the habit of using the porta-potty.'

"They all thought that was cool, so they quit teasing me after a while. I didn't have to prove anything to anyone.

"When we would get back from the fields, everyone would go their own way. I got myself a small boarding room, which I would pay by the week as I had done earlier.

"When my money ran out, which didn't last too long, I started sleeping in the park on park benches or under trees.

"When it would rain or become too cold, I would find the city library and stay there and study. I tried to keep up with some of my schoolwork, so I joined a study after work. It was fun learning again.

"I enjoyed working with the guys. I began to have several friends. Sometimes they would ask me to join them in going to the bar after work, but I was able to say no; I told them that I had to study. They couldn't believe that I would want to do something as goofy as that, but they respected it. I really did not want to get to close to them in case they would suspect that I was really a girl.

"Then after five months, the orange season was suddenly over. The man in the store gave us a large bag of oranges to thank us for our help for the season, but this didn't help much. I just knew that I didn't have a job again. I only had the last day's pay, as all the other money I had was entirely gone. I really was a street person now.

"Most of the men went back to their homes or on to another place, hoping to find more work somewhere else. I didn't know what to do. I knew that I had to find work soon or I would have to quit eating. I was already living on the street.

"I was becoming depressed. I knew that I needed some help or guidance. But where will I be able to get this? I remembered that God loved me. 'Please continue to love me and help me get a job or find a way, if you are still out there.' I prayed that night as I crawled up on my park bench and went to sleep. Dreaming of family and people around me loving me, I didn't want to wake up. I also dreamt that I finally found the truth and was free. But the truth I had found in my dream was still an illusion.

"Oh, how I wished so many time that I could find you and our father."

Paul was overwhelmed with the story Tiffany was telling him as he said, "I feel so bad what you have had to go through. I am so thankful that we have finally met and you can feel our love for you. Please tell me how you came about finding us."

Chapter 14

In Need of Help!

"I hadn't been able to get a job since the orange-picking season had finished one week earlier. Without money enough to pay for a roof over my head, I was forced to sleep on park benches for several months. My last meager wage had been absorbed. I counted and noticed I only had two dollars in change left. I knew that I needed to find work or something very quick! I would be seventeen soon and thought I was really becoming a loser. I didn't have a job, slept on park benches at night, and begged for food during the day. How desperate I had become. I started getting more depressed.

"I didn't know what I was going to do that morning as I popped into my usual dingy cafe where the waitresses knew me and would usually offer me a free glass of iced tea.

"As I was cooling off, sipping, and savoring my tea, I noticed an open newspaper on the table next to me. The headline jumped out at me. DO YOU NEED HELP? *Boy, do I need help!* But what really caught my attention was a picture of a man in his late twenties under the capture. I gasped as I said, 'He looks just like me!' I was so shocked, I blurted out loud.

"The waitress standing nearby came over to me. As she read over my shoulder, she said, 'He does look like you, only a little neater. Who is he anyway?'

"I read further, 'Pastor Paul of the Church of Christ in Buena Vista is starting a home for young homeless people. He is dedicating this home to his sister Tiffany, whom he has been looking for fourteen years and has not seen or heard from her in all this time.'

"My heart suddenly started to pound, I gasped. 'I think that I may be that sister,' I said without remembering that I was still masquerading around, disguised as Samuel.

"'Yeah, right!' the waitress said. 'If you are this guy's sister, then I'm the queen of Sheba's son.'

"'I think I'm going to give this guy a call and see if I can get some answers and maybe some help,' I said, ignoring the waitress's comments as I quickly got up and walked over to the phone. I was preoccupied with what was going through my head: *This may truly be my brother, which I hadn't seen since I was three years old.*

"My hands were shaking as I placed one of my last coins into the telephone. 'Please, God, if you are really out there, let this be my brother,' I prayed as I dialed the phone number listed in the paper.

"'Hello, this is Pastor Paul, may I help you?' came over the voice from the other end of the phone.

"My mind was racing and my heart was pounding as I struggled for the right words. I didn't want to make a mistake with such an important call. "I . . . I read your article in the *Miami Herald,* about your place for young homeless people. I think I can use your help,' I stammered but finally got through.

"'You are certainly welcome to come here, we will help you. Can you tell me your name?' Pastor Paul continued.

"'M . . . my name is T . . . Tiffany,' I finally was able to stammer out. "I saw your picture and I . . . I think I might be your s . . . sister,' I continued to stutter, thinking, *What if this is a hoax, and I'm making a fool of myself, I had been looking for my brother and father for so many years that this might be another dead-end.*

"A gasp was heard at the other end and nothing for a long time, when your voice came back, it was shaking, as you asked, 'Tiffany, is this really you? Are you really my sister? I have been looking and praying for you since we were separated fourteen years ago. Are . . . are you okay? I am very anxious to see you. Where are you, right now? Is there a Greyhound bus depot near by?'

"When I explained to you, where I was and the closest bus depot, I hated to tell you that I didn't have any money to get there."

"I could hear the love and graciousness, as you said, 'I will make arrangements for you to pick up a ticket at the bus depot nearby, and I will meet you at the restaurant next to the station. See you tomorrow. Ah . . . I . . . I love you.'

"I was sobbing as I sensed, that you could really be my brother 'T . . . thank you, I am very anxious to meet you and feel that you are really my brother. I . . . I love you also. Goodbye, I will see you tomorrow.' After hanging up the phone, I continued to sob,as I thought, *I have waited for so many years to hear those wonderful words.*

"I immediately went into the bathroom. I was anxious to get rid of my disguise and go back to being a girl again, but when I looked in the mirror and was wiping my smudged face, it brought me back to reality. *I need to keep this disguise in case Frank or one of his thugs will be looking for me at the bus depot.* I knew that I could only let go of my guard when I was safe with you, my brother, again. I prayed to God what I hoped he would take for a prayer, 'God if you truly love me, please let this be my brother.'

"When I returned to my table, the waitress asked, 'What did you find out?'

"'Yeah, I think that I may be Pastor Paul's sister. He wants me to come to Orlando tomorrow morning,' I said with excitement as I completely forgot that I was still disguised as Samuel.

"The waitress was stunned. As I was counting out the pennies for my meal, she said, 'Samuel, I'll never understand how you can be that guy's sister.'

"I smiled as I said something that suddenly came to my mind, 'Someday, you will know the truth and it will set you free. I am starting to feel this freedom is coming to me.'

"The waitress looked puzzled, but a calm came to her face as she said, 'You are getting weirder by the minute, but I have to give you credit. Good luck to you.'

"As I headed for the door, I said to her, 'Thanks for all of your encouragement, and remember to seek after the truth. This seeking has always kept me going. Goodbye.'

"I waved and ran all the way to the bus stop. I planned to sleep there so I would be in time for the flight at 9 a.m. I was excited to finally be able to see light on my dreary situation.

"My heart was pounding as I entered into the bus station. The distance I ran was longer than I had thought, but I had managed to get there without getting lost. It was getting near the time when the buses were coming in; the people were starting to congregate. I managed to move around so I could stay away from the general public. I found a corner where no one seemed to care if I was there or not. I didn't want anyone to kick me out for loitering. I managed to get some rest. That night, I dreamed of finding my brother and also my dad. Somehow, in my dream, Dad looked just like Stan.

"The next morning, I went into the rest room and cleaned up the best I could. I put on my cleanest jeans and another baggy shirt. I went to the ticket station and got the ticket you sent. I was so thrilled that things were finally coming together. I remembered that I always gave you a treat when you helped me, so I had saved one orange just to give to you when I met you. I knew you were going to be there for me once more.

"'Now we are together, and I have never been so happy in all my life,' Tiffany said as she continued to hang on to her brother's arm, tears of happiness present.

Paul was also pouring out the tears as he said, "I'm so very sorry you had to go through all of these trials, but I know that God had kept you safe through it all and that you have become a stronger person because of it. Let us pray and give thanks for all he has done for us. They all bowed their heads, and Pastor Paul prayed, "Lord, you have been so very faithful to your children. We sometimes don't deserve your wonderful love and kindness. We know that you are the only one who can make our lives meaningful. Thank you for my sister and your wonderful caring hands during her ordeal and bringing her safely back home to us. God, also help her find and know that the meaning of "The truth that will set her free" is in you all the time. Amen."

Chapter 15

Tiffany's Nightmares

After Tiffany found her brother, her world changed for the better. She still faced the fact that Frank and Harry were still lurking around out there somewhere waiting to pounce on her if she let her guard down. She was fearful of that but did not want to worry Paul. He was being so very nice to her since she had come to stay with him and his family. This was the family she had wanted for so long; she never wanted to lose them. She knew that Paul would help her, but she was afraid it would affect the situation. She just wanted it all to go away. She tried so hard to let go of these fears on her own, but she just couldn't do it.

Paul would see this suffering and pain from Tiffany's past. Every time he would look in his sister's dark eyes, he would pray, "Please, Lord, help us that someday we will be able to see Tiffany's eyes bright and shiny again."

Anytime Tiffany would try to do something with her new family, she would have dreadful fears of running into Frank or one of his goons. Harry was out of jail now, and he had also threatened her. Oh, how she hated those men. She knew that her hatred was possibly causing her frightful nightmares, which she had on many nights and were increasing with more frequency.

Tiffany's nightmares were always about Frank and her stepfather Harry both chasing her. Most of the time, they would almost catch her, and then Stan would show up to protect her. On occasion, they would grab her, and she would start to scream out in her sleep. This was becoming more frequent.

One night, as Tiffany was kicking and struggling to get away from the bad guys in her dream, she let out a blood-curdling scream. Paul came running. He could see Tiffany all curled up in a ball in her bed, with sweat draining down her face; she was having another nightmare.

He said with brotherly love and holding her in his arms, "Won't you tell me what you are so frightened about? Maybe I can help you. We all love you. You are safe here."

Tiffany could feel her brother's comforting arms and blurted out her deepest fear, "My mother's ex-boyfriend Frank is out of jail and out there somewhere, and I'm afraid he is going to find me. He threatened to kill me; the police think that he killed my mother. He keeps evading the police. My friend Stan has helped me to get away from him once, but now I keep thinking he'll find me again. I don't want your family to get hurt because of me."

Tears welled in Paul's eyes as he was shaken by his sister's words. Paul hugged Tiffany as he said, "I'll never let anyone hurt you like that again. We will find out about Frank and what is going on. I want you to let Stan and me work on this for you." Paul wanted so badly to tell Tiffany the secret he had to keep for Stan's sake.

The next day, Paul checked with the police department in Pittsburgh and found out the good news.

He was anxious to tell Tiffany that evening when he got home from work.

He sat down beside Tiffany and said with eagerness, "Frank is locked up in the Pittsburgh jail awaiting trial for murder, drug dealing, and other multiple crimes. His trial is coming up soon, and the letter you gave to the police will help convict him. There was enough evidence in that letter and other evidences the police and FBI have been able to bring against him. He will be put away for a long time. I don't want you to have to worry now."

Tiffany hugged Paul and, with relief, blurted out, "Thank you so much, I love you."

That night, as Tiffany lay in her bed, a thought kept going over and over in her head, *Could there be some relationship between Paul and Stan? They both have the same name. I can't think about that now. I'm so happy just being here and safe. I have that name now also.* She snickered as she fell asleep.

Tiffany was so relieved that Frank was in jail and she could finally settle down. She wanted so much to please her new family, so she decided to finish high school. This was not the easiest chore, as she hadn't been to school since she was fourteen years old. She was glad that she had studied some while working in Miami, but at seventeen, it was embarrassing to be going back to school with thirteen and fourteen-year-old children. The kids would tease her, but the love she received from her family made up for any wise cracks she got from the other students.

Tiffany loved going to church each Sunday with her family. Church felt so comforting. It would bring back the memory the first time she had ever stepped into a church with her friend Anne so many years ago. She could still remember the words the pastor said that were set so deeply into her heart at that time: the truth will set you free. Tiffany was still searching for this truth.

Chapter 16

The Truth Is Found to Set Us Free

Tiffany was finally getting her life straightened around now that the fear of Frank and his goons were gone. She settled down and finished school and was able to pass with honors and graduate with the class. She had plans to go to college for nursing and applied at a college in Orlando. She got accepted and was to start the summer quarter.

She was so excited; she wanted to talk to someone and decided to call Sue. When Tiffany dialed her number, the operator at the other end said, "This number has been permanently disconnected."

Tiffany, concerned, decided to call the Delos Cafe and see if Bill was there. Maybe he would know where Sue was. When Tiffany dialed the number, someone different answered saying, "Wayne here."

Tiffany stammered and asked, "Does Bill still work there?"

"Oh yes; he is on his honeymoon. Can I ask who is calling?" Wayne asked.

"Yes, this is Tiffany Anderson. I used to work for Bill; I was wondering if I could come back to work. I'm going to college and would like to work in the evening, if that is possible," Tiffany said a little prayer that she would get the job.

"Oh yes, Bill talked about you a lot. He told me if you called, I was supposed to tell you that you are welcome to come back and work anytime. In fact, I have an evening position open right now. Are you interested?" he asked excitedly.

Tiffany's heart flipped as she said, "Yes, I would be over in two hours to talk with you. Thank you so very much. By the way, whom did Bill marry?" she asked, hoping that he would say Sue. When he did, she was so thrilled for them both.

"I'll see you in a couple hours then," Wayne said.

"I'll be there," Tiffany said.

When Tiffany was ready to leave, Paul offered to drive her to the college campus. She got her room, deposited her clothes in it, and Paul then drove her over to the Delos Cafe.

As they walked in, all her old friends gave them a warm greeting. Tiffany introduced Paul to the workers that she had worked with before.

He smiled sweetly and said, "You all are so lucky to have my sweet sister work with you." Then he winked at Tiffany as he gave her a goodbye hug. "You come for dinner now, when you have a break, you hear. I love you. Goodbye. It is nice to meet all of you," he said as he walked out the door.

"You really have a nice brother," they all commented.

"I know. It took us a long time to find each other, but he's worth it all," Tiffany said with a feeling of pride and happiness, which she was sure showed in her eyes.

The next evening, Tiffany began her job. "They still have my uniforms waiting for me. They must have known that I was coming back," she said to one of her friends. "I sure am happy being back," she commented.

Tiffany worked all that week. By the time Friday rolled around, she felt that she was right back into the rhythm of working and loving it.

That night when she was almost finished for the evening, she felt someone staring at her from behind her back. As she whirled around, there stood Jim with a big smile on his handsome face and with that wonderful sparkle in his eyes. "Oh, Tiffany, is that really you? I have missed you so much. You look wonderful!" he said as he came over to Tiffany and gave her a big hug.

"I am so happy to see you, and you also look great," Tiffany said with happiness and excitement. She was thrilled to see him again.

"How about going for a cup of coffee when you get off work? I will wait for you if you will be getting off soon," he said with those wonderful eyes and his beautiful grin.

Tiffany was thinking, *Oh how I have missed you, especially that wonderful smile.*

Then she said, "That would be great. I will get off in an hour."

"Hey, you can go now, we'll finish up here," Mary, Tiffany's co-worker, said as she gave her a wink.

"Well, all right, let's go," Jim said to Tiffany as he took her arm and led her out the door.

Tiffany could feel the butterflies in her stomach as Jim took her arm. He was so wonderful.

Jim took Tiffany to a restaurant near the campus. They sat and talked for several hours.

Tiffany told him of some of her experiences and how she finally found her brother. When she explained about dressing like a boy so Frank wouldn't find her, Jim laughed, then he turned serious as he said, "You have really been through a lot, but I have to give you credit; you made it."

Being anxious to find how he was doing, Tiffany asked, "Enough about me. What are you doing now? You must be almost through with school?"

He said, "Right now, I am working as an intern at the local hospital and plan to get my masters in a few weeks, and then I have plans to go on to get my Ph.D. Did I hear right that you are going to college for nursing? That is wonderful. Maybe we will someday work together," he said with that beautiful smile.

"Yes, but it will be a few years before I get finished; I just started." Suddenly realizing how late it was getting, Tiffany said, "I hate to have to say this, but it is getting late. I have to be in class early in the morning," Tiffany said, hating to have to leave Jim.

"Oh my, it is late. I'm so sorry for keeping you up so late," Jim said as he looked at his watch. "I'll walk you to your room; it's just across the street, right?"

"How did you know where I lived?" Tiffany was taken by surprise.

"I've been so anxious to see you I talked to Wayne, and he gave me the information. I hope that doesn't bother you," he said, lowering his head as if he had been disobedient.

"I guess I say that is a compliment that you were anxious to see me," Tiffany said as her heart made another flip-flop. "We better get going."

As they walked Tiffany back to her room, Jim sheepishly asked her, "Would you be interested in coming to church with me Sunday morning? I could pick you up at 9 a.m., then we can stop for breakfast before church."

Tiffany had almost forgotten that she had planned to go to her brother's for dinner. She then said, encouraged, "I will go with you if you will come to my brother's with me for dinner after. I would love for them to meet you."

Tiffany could tell Jim was delighted by the big grin he had on his face. "Why, yes, that would be great. It's a date then. See you at 9 a.m. Sunday. I sure have missed you," Jim said again as he bent down and kissed Tiffany on the lips. Tiffany had never been kissed like that before, and her heart started pounding. She was in seventh heaven.

When she came to, she could feel her face flushing, and the feeling went down to her toes. She then said caringly, "Thanks so much for everything. I'll see you Sunday morning. Goodbye."

That night, Tiffany went to bed dreaming of sweet Jim. I think I might be falling for him. She suddenly felt the urge to thank God as she prayed, "Thank you, God, for bringing Jim back into my life."

The next day, Tiffany got up and hurried off to class. After her classes, she headed to work. It being Saturday night, she was busy. She was glad, but that didn't help to get Jim off her mind.

Then around 7:30 p.m., just as everyone was cleaning up ready to close, Tiffany spied a shadow lurking around outside the door. She let out a gasp as she recognized the person coming into the restaurant as Harry, her stepfather. She recognized him by his ugly piercing eerie eyes.

She knew that she had to get away quickly before he saw her, if he hadn't already. She quickly said to her co-worker, "Could you finish up here? I think I see someone coming in here whom I don't want to tangle with. I'll tell you about it later. Thanks."

She grabbed her purse and slipped out the back door and started running down the alley. She was hoping and praying that Harry had not seen her.

She realized that he had indeed seen her, as she heard the loud thunderous steps running behind her. She was frightened. She didn't know what he was capable of doing. She knew that he was a very angry and an unstable person. He might even have a gun. She didn't know what to do.

Her mind was in turmoil as she continued to run as fast as she could to get away from the loud breathing behind her coming closer. As she continued to race down the dark street, she didn't dare look back. She started praying, hoping that God was still around somewhere to help her out. "God, please help me once more."

All of a sudden, a church loomed in front of her. She rushed into the crowd that was going into the church and swiftly went and sat down in one of the front pews. She was afraid to turn around. She wasn't sure if Harry had followed her into the church; she sure wasn't going to look back and have him see her. Tiffany crouched down between the other parishioners and bowed down. She figured that Harry would be waiting outside for her, as he hated churches.

Tiffany felt safe in the church. This feeling was always with her when she was in a church for some reason. Suddenly, the service started with praise and singing. Tiffany got up and sang with the crowd but wasn't sure of what she was singing and praising about. She had heard most of these songs from Paul's church and was familiar with the praising, but somehow, this was different.

Then the pastor said, "There are many people in this congregation who need to know the truth that will set them free."

"Wow, that's me!" Tiffany almost said out loud. This really got her attention.

The pastor continued, "John 8:32 reads, 'You shall know the truth, and the truth will set you free.'" Tiffany's ears perked up; she had waited to hear these words for years to find out the truth. She was so wrapped up in these words that she completely forgot about Harry.

The pastor continued, "In John 8:33, Jesus is saying, 'I tell you the truth. Everyone who sins is a slave to sin, and a slave has no permanent place in the family, but a son belongs to it forever. So if the son Jesus sets you free, you will be free indeed.'" The pastor continued, "John 14:6, Jesus said, 'I am the way, the truth, and the light. No one comes to the father except through me.'" A bulb went off in Tiffany's head. She suddenly realized that Jesus was the truth and that he was the truth she had been searching for all her life.

The pastor continued, "I have a revelation. There are people in this congregation who are in need of this truth, and I want them to come forward."

Tiffany was out of her seat, with no help of her own. She felt as if she floated up and was placed in front of the altar. She knelt down as tears streamed down her face. She prayed, "Please forgive all of my sins and come into my heart." As she said these words, she felt a burden lifted off of her. The pastor came over and said, "Now, you must forgive all those who have harmed you in any way."

Hey, wait a minute, forgive those who have harmed me, was her first thought, but in her heart, she knew that Jesus would help her with this assignment. She had such a desire to be obedient to God.

Tiffany was praying with head bowed as she walked back to her seat. She had to walk toward the back of the church and, wouldn't you know it, ran smack-dab into Harry.

Tiffany thought, *You don't waste any time, do you, Lord?* She stepped back and stared at Harry. She couldn't believe that suddenly she had no fear of him; instead, she noticed something different in his eyes as she blurted out, "I forgive you for everything. Please forgive me also, and I love you." She certainly didn't plan to say that, but apparently, the Lord did.

All of a sudden, tears fell from Harry's eyes as he looked at her and asked, "How can you say that after all the terrible things I have done to you?"

"I have finally found the truth of Jesus, and he has set me free," Tiffany said with confidence and love. She felt completely free of any fear or hate toward this man.

"How can I get the truth so I may be set free?" he asked as tears continued to flow down his cheeks.

"Go and ask Jesus to forgive you for all of your sins and ask him into your heart. You will then also be set free," Jesus said through Tiffany.

Before Tiffany knew it, Harry was slowly moving forward with his head bowed, weeping greatly. She watched as he knelt before the altar. She knew that he also would be set free.

Tiffany then waited for him to come back. When he came back to his seat, she could see a sparkle in his eyes and a complete different look on his face that she had never seen before. She knew that Harry had given his life to Jesus, just as she had done.

As they walked out of the church arm in arm, Harry asked, "Will I see you in church Sunday?"

"Yes. Maybe you would like to come with my friend Jim and me for dinner at my brother's after church tomorrow?" Tiffany asked as they parted.

"I would really like that," Harry said. "I'll see you tomorrow then."

Tiffany ran the total way to her room; she was so happy. "Thank you, Lord, for saving me again today and for showing me the truth that set me free. You are that truth."

When she got to her room, she couldn't wait to talk to Paul. She picked up the phone and dialed his house. She was so excited to be able to tell him her good news. She said, "Hi, Paul. Would it be okay if I could bring another person along with Jim and myself when we come for dinner tomorrow? I have a wonderful surprise for you."

"That will be fine, I'll have Maria set another place," Paul said, and then he continued, "I also have a wonderful surprise for you tomorrow, see you at noon then." Tiffany thought, *Now what could that be? I know that he will be happy about my surprise.*

Sunday morning, Jim was at the door right at 9 a.m., just as planned. The two went out to breakfast as Tiffany related to him all the things that had happened the night before. Jim smiled and said, "I'm so happy that you have finally found what you have been searching for all you life. God is good, isn't he?"

"You're right on that one." Tiffany agreed as she realized that Jim was already a Christian. They then set off for church. As they entered the church, Harry was waiting in the back pew, looking very spiffy.

As Tiffany introduced Jim to Harry, she noticed Harry had the warmest, sincere smile as he extended his hand toward Jim. She was feeling very peaceful as she sat through the service, praising and thanking God. She enjoyed every minute of it.

After the service, Jim drove his old Ford, with Tiffany by his side, to her brother's place in Buena Vista. Harry decided to follow them with his own rental car, as he had to get back to the airport tonight. They all arrived at Paul's shortly after twelve o'clock. When they drove into the driveway, Tiffany noticed a familiar car in the driveway. Her first thought was, *I wonder if that is Stan's car. Maybe that is my surprise, but why is he here? There's something going on here.* She couldn't wait to see Stan again. She was hoping that it would be him.

Paul answered as Tiffany rang the doorbell. "Hi, Paul. It is sure wonderful to see you again. I would like you to meet my friend Jim." As Paul shook Jim's hand, he said, "I'm happy to meet you. Tiffany has said a lot about you." Jim gave Tiffany a special look then, which made her blush.

Tiffany changed the subject and said, "This is my stepfather, Harry, and he is part of the surprise I told you about."

Paul had a weird, unsure look on his face. Seeing it, Harry chimed in and said, "I am a new person, since I have found the truth, and now I am free from sin. I belong to God's family. It is so wonderful to be whole in this way," he said with excitement.

Tiffany couldn't keep her surprise inside any longer. She blurted it out, "Yes, the other surprise is that I also have found the truth that I have been searching for all my life, and I am finally free. It feels so good."

Paul knew exactly what Tiffany and Harry were talking about. He was so happy for them both. He said as he hugged them all, including Jim, "It is really wonderful to have that feeling and to know that you will have eternal life also."

Tiffany turned around and looked into the dining room. There stood Stan. She ran over to him and gave him a big hug. "This is your surprise," Paul said as the rest came into the room. "This is your real dad," he said with excitement in his eyes.

Tiffany was ecstatic, her eyes blurred with tears of happiness. When she finally got her composure, she said, "I had suspected the possibility – even hoped and prayed for this – but never imagined that it would really happen. I am so happy to have you as my real dad. Thank you, Jesus, for bringing me to the complete truth. You have made this day the greatest day of my life." She prayed as Stan stood with his arms around her with the proudest look on his face and the most sincere smile.

He then said, "Tiffany, I wanted to tell you I was your dad for so long, but I couldn't until Frank was safely behind bars. I didn't want you to be hurt by what I had to do."

"I'm just so happy I know now," she said, tears still coming. Then she remembered that she had forgotten Jim and Harry in all of her excitement. "Oh my golly, I forgot to introduce you to two other important people in my life. Harry and Jim, I want you to meet the real father I am so happy to have. Stan – oh I mean, Dad, I want you to meet Jim, my friend, and Harry, my stepfather. You probably heard about our great news?" She continued to say as she looked back at her dad and smiled with pride. "I am a new person and I know the truth and I am free."

Stan then said, "I heard, and I think that's the most wonderful news you can give us."

They all held hands as Paul said the dinner prayer. "Thank you, God, for all the wonderful things you have brought to light, and especially for Jesus, the truth that has set everyone free."

"Yes, God, you have certainly done that for us. Thank you, sir," Tiffany chimed in as they all sat down to a wonderful dinner. "Now, we are all one big happy family with God as our father."

Tiffany felt so very proud as she looked around at her family. Little Stan and Allison were beaming. Jim and Harry smiled at her as if they could sense the love she felt in all the people in the room, especially her brother and her real dad, who were the most wonderful of all.

After dinner and the dishes done, the family settled into the family room to visit. Stan said, "By the way, the FBI finally got all of Frank's men in jail. The letter your mother wrote secured their stay in jail for a lifetime. We were finally able to get many of the higher people above Frank, which we could never get before, because of the information your mom had. We have to thank you, Tiffany, for this help."

"How did you ever find him?" Tiffany asked, although thankful they had.

"We were able to catch Frank when he went to the modeling place you had worked in. Because you were able to slip away from them again, Hank had to call Frank, who was so angry that he came there to try and find you. We were waiting for him and was able to nab him and all his thugs," Stan continued.

"But how did you find out that I had worked there and that Frank had bought it?" Tiffany asked with curiosity.

"When you called Sue about the job, she called me, as she was worried about you getting into a situation you maybe couldn't get out of. I sent a fellow down there and found out that Frank had bought the business. Tom was a very brilliant man. He had canceled all the model contracts before the takeover so the new owners had no contracts or models to use. These people used these modeling agencies and the models they took over as a prostitute business. You're very lucky that Tom did not continue your contract; otherwise you would have had to stay and work out your contract with these men. Oh, I almost forgot, Tom says to say hi to you. He's back in his old shop again and said if you ever need a modeling job, look him up. He and Sandy got married a few weeks ago," he continued.

"I am so happy for them and for the way things turned out," Tiffany said with relief.

"By the way, what happened to you after you left Tom? We lost you completely," Stan asked with puzzlement.

"You wouldn't want to know," Tiffany said as she laughed and winked at Paul and Jim.

The evening was so wonderful that everyone hated to leave. Harry had to go back to Pittsburgh. He said, "I have many amends to make and things to work out to clean up my life. I know that the Lord has plans for me. I will keep in contact with you." He directed this to Tiffany. "Thanks for the wonderful evening. Tiffany, I feel so fortunate that you are able to completely forgive me for all the bad things I had done to you. I have been able to repent all these things to God. I want you to know also that I had loved your mom very much, but feeling so inadequate, I started drinking and starting doing the dumb things that I did. I have learned since that drinking is not a good thing to do. In fact, I was coming to see you to ask for your forgiveness when I came to your job. I should have known that you would be frightened of me. I will be thankful for the rest of my life for the ways things turned out. I do not have any more guilt. I am free."

"I am very glad that Tiffany asked me here so I could meet all of you wonderful people," he said to the rest. As he left in his car to go back to the airport, Tiffany knew that the Lord had plans for him as he also had for her.

Stan got up and said, "I have to leave also to return to my job. Don't any of you be a stranger now when you get to Pittsburgh? I have met a wonderful lady and plan to be married in about a year, so be prepared for an invitation. I sure would like my family there." He said with a radiant smile directed at Tiffany and Paul

"I am so happy for you. You be sure and let us know when. I'll be there for sure. I'm not afraid of coming back to Pittsburgh now that all the bad memories are gone," Tiffany said, filled with gratitude

Jim and Tiffany were the last to leave. They said their goodbyes and took off in Jim's old 1989 Ford. As they drove back to Orlando, Jim took a different route. He had this mischievous grin on his face.

"Where are we going?" Tiffany asked, starting to feel thrilled to be with Jim alone, finally.

"We are going to just take a scenic route, is that okay?" he answered with a question as they drove out toward the ocean. The ocean had a beautiful reddened glaze reflected from the sun as it went down in the west. This beauty dazzled the two as they sat on the beach watching it.

All of a sudden, Jim said as he placed his arms around Tiffany, "I have loved you since the first day I met you. You were only fourteen then, I believe. I didn't know it at that time. You have turned into such a beauty and a real lady. I am so thankful that God is in your life. I would like to spend more time with you. I want you to be my girl."

Tiffany was thrilled as she heard these words. "I have a long time to go to school yet, you may not want to wait for me that long, but if you will, I would love to be your girl."

That summer was a wonderful one for Tiffany. She was the happiest she had ever been. Jim and she were not able to spend too much time together, as they were both busy with their schools and occupations, but they kept in contact over the phone.

One day, as she met with Jim for dinner, she said, "I got a letter from my dad, guess what?"

"Your dad has invited you to his wedding," Jim stated.

"Yes that, but there's more. You remember Harry? He is working as a prison chaplain, and can you guess where? He is chaplain at the prison where Frank is. Isn't God good? God has saved Harry, now he is using Harry to save Frank."

Seeing the sparkle and beauty in Tiffany's eyes, Jim said, "God certainly is good. Look how he has given you the truth and given you a new life."

"Yeah, you're right. I now know exactly who I am, and I like being a child of God."

Note: Bible verses were taken from the New International Version of the Bible.